D0895327

YOUNG IRELANDERS

ALSO BY THE SAME AUTHOR

Sunless
Julius Winsome
Schopenhauer's Telescope

YOUNG IRELANDERS

STORIES

GERARD DONOVAN

3 1336 07919 9619

THE OVERLOOK PRESS
Woodstock & New York

This edition first published in the United States in 2008 by
The Overlook Press, Peter Mayer Publishers, Inc.
Woodstock & New York

WOODSTOCK:
One Overlook Drive
Woodstock, NY 12498
www.overlookpress.com
[for individual orders, bulk and special sales, contact our Woodstock office]

NEW YORK:
141 Wooster Street
New York, NY 10012

Cataloging-in-Publication Data is available from the Library of Congress

Book design and type formatting by Bernard Schleifer
Manufactured in the United States of America
ISBN 978-1-59020-030-8
10 9 8 7 6 5 4 3 2 1

for Fiona Carrick

CONTENTS

Frailty, thy name is man

MORNING SWIMMERS

IN THE FIRST WEEK OF MAY, before the water in Galway Bay changed to a mild summer blue, Eric Hartman and John Berry drove to Jim's house and announced that they had gone swimming that morning, at eight o'clock, by the diving tower at the end of the promenade in Salthill. The three men had grown up together and still lived in the same town, though in recent years Jim had seen them less, or as they put it, they had seen less of Jim.

It was still early morning and Jim walked the kitchen in pajamas and crooked glasses, bringing cups of tea to the white table.

Eric said, You should come with us, make it three.

John said, Yes, the water's cold, the concrete is cold, but once you're in the water it's not too bad.

They said nothing more as Jim sat with his cup. He scratched the hair that still felt for the pillow he hurried from when he heard the doorbell. It had been five or six weeks since he'd seen either of them. This was the way with even boyhood friends: sooner or later another life always comes with its bags, even in the late years.

Jim said, I'm not a man for cold water, but I heard the bay is warmer in January than summer, with the Gulf Stream from Mexico.

Eric said, Always the man for facts. Are you up for it then?

Jim looked at the floor between his feet and saw the tower. It was a cold place, the tower and the concrete shelter at the end of the promenade, completely open to the elements, completely without comfort in the face of the strong wind off the bay. And that solitary journey to a cold dunk in the frigid water drew solitary people to it every morning. As a child he watched the old bony swimmers leap into the water and swim around the base of the tower and run shivering for the towels they draped on the railings. One man used to leap straight from the sea onto his black bike, cycling home instead to change, stopping wet on the way to buy a newspaper. Perhaps all those memories made him want to agree to go with them, or perhaps the recent loneliness that visited him in the mornings had taken to staying a little longer by the week.

And so it came to pass that at eight in the morning, four times a week through the summer and well into autumn, the three of them swam in the waters of the Atlantic, fast pink arms in the churn of the dark seas.

Today Jim had come twenty minutes early. The water was slate gray and a blustery wind seemed to push the sunlight off the boulders that ringed the tower. He had not slept well, and as he drove along the seaside he saw rain showers blowing in from the Aran Islands and knew he did not want to wait for the other two. The routine had taken over the excitement, he understood that, but lately their conversation shared the same fate as the time trapped in his watch, it always came around to a point where it used to be. He parked his car farther down the promenade than usual and walked the extra distance to warm himself. Because the November sunrise had found the clear part of the sky, he wanted to swim while the sun could shine on his skin, even a sun without heat, any sun, because this time of year was unforgiving: you ran in and got the thing done. But if he kept coming, doing this, perhaps by spring he would feel differently.

He undressed down to the swimming trunks he wore underneath and picked his way on flat feet across the stones to the water, found a patch free of seaweed, bent at the knees and launched himself. The cold clamped him at the head and the chest and dragged ice along his body as he entered fully the green silence, opening his eyes to the salt and the waving seaweed, the fat tendrils' ballet in a slow current. He thrashed his arms, twisted his neck, rose to the surface and kicked his legs until a seed of heat burned at the numbness. He made a tight circle around the tower and hauled himself onto a rock, gasping and saying incomprehensible things just to ward off the brutal chill. A gust sliced spray off the rocks after him as he grabbed his bag and ran to the shelter to change. He placed firmly in his mind the dry promise of the towel, the second sun gleaming from the dashboard in the car on the way home, the hot shower of water from pipes.

Inside the shelter, he took the towel and entered the only cubicle even though he was the only one there. Jim liked the ounce of privacy. He wrapped the ends of the towel in his fists and see-sawed it along his back with his toes curled off the damp concrete, dabbed his chest and legs, noticed the strings of blue veins under the skin. He threw the towel down and reached for the underpants. That was the good thing about the harsh concrete of this place: you didn't want to hang about and think.

He was drying his feet when he heard his name spoken at the door of the shelter.

Remember what Jim said—last July, was it?

What did he say?

Jim smiled as he recognised the voices of his friends. He dredged the toes of his left foot with the towel.

John said, Don't say anything, is that Jim's car parked outside?

I'll look, Eric said. No, he's not there.

Jim had a hand on the cubicle door to push it open and tell them he had beaten them to the swim, but then John shouted, Listen, today is going to be the best day of our lives!

Eric laughed, Will you keep it down, will you? He could be along any second.

Jim stopped. Was that something he had said once? He said that once. He should put his trousers on first before leaving the cubicle.

I mean, John said, he's out there on the rocks and says that to us about the best day of our lives. What was that all about?

I could hardly stop myself from laughing out loud, Eric said. He stands in his wet trunks with his arms up in the air and says, 'Look at the clear water, the sun in the clouds', and then he says—

Don't—

'Christ, lads, isn't it great to be alive!'

Inside the cubicle Jim pulled his trousers on. The rest of his clothes were in the plastic shopping bag outside the cubicle. He couldn't very well walk out now to get his shirt and socks. His friends were talking about him, and they would be embarrassed. He would be embarrassed.

John got his breath back. I felt like saying, 'The best day? We're going swimming, Jim. What are you doing?'

I wouldn't mind but he's the one who got winded, Eric said, tried to go out a hundred yards and ends up floundering. Lucky the man didn't get blown out to sea altogether. Thinks he's still a young fellow.

Inside the cubicle, Jim smiled. They were talking about him behind his back, and he was listening behind theirs. He'd wait another minute before springing the surprise. They'd all laugh about it later in the bar, a little friendly elbowing. How many get to hear what their friends say about them.

As he waited, carefully silent in the cubicle, Jim remembered that day of his extra-long swim: it was midsummer and he felt brave enough to explore, to go farther, stretch the circle out in a wider radius to the bigger waves and be helpless and brave in all that water. He was tired of the same path his friends dug out of the waves to follow. It was something he decided at the moment he dove in and so could not tell the others, who always swam as a pair a little behind him. He took a left turn and in two minutes was already far enough out that the tower had shrunk two or three inches and his friends were half the size. It was more than he bargained for. How tired he got! He didn't say anything at first, but when the cramp tugged at his calf, he wanted to call out to the others, but they might laugh at him or not notice the call coming from an unexpected place, so far to their left where no one ever swam, and so he treaded water to get his breath and watched his friends circle the tower and pick themselves out of the sea. Then he felt the first tug of a different current push him out a few inches more, an indifferent hand pushing him out into the open and anonymous sea and beyond the magnet of the tower. The terror of those inches! The sea yawned under him. He kicked and thrashed his way parallel to the shore until the tugging stopped and he was able to head for the beach, coming from the waves fifty yards downshore. He wound his way back to the shelter along the sharp rocks in the surge of sun and the relief that he was on dry ground, and when he reached the tower, his friends were already in the shelter, but his relief had turned into joy. He stood on the flat lukewarm stone, and that was when he shouted that today would be the best day of their lives, that it was great to be alive after all.

Jim buttoned his trousers. Outside the cubicle, his friends were not finished with him.

Eric said, Ever think Jim was a little, you know, off?

As in?

Don't know really. Off.

Daft? John said.

Eric said, Daft. Good daft, I mean.

No wonder his wife—

Wait. I want to hear, but check again first.

Jim moved away from the door. No wonder his wife what? He hung the towel at his shoulders.

Eric's voice sounded again after footsteps: Nothing. He's late today. Maybe he's not coming.

We better get in and swim, looks dark out in the bay.

Jim heard bags rustle and shoes thud as they undressed. If he opened the door now, he would mortify his two friends. At this point he would gladly have taken the embarrassment he passed on previously. Best to wait until they left the shelter for the swim and then to get his bag, dress quickly, go outside and wave at them as if he'd just arrived. Two swims for him today.

She's not bad-looking at all, John said.

A quiet one, though.

Heard she's seeing some fellow from Dublin, some archeologist or other.

Jim leaned against the wall of the changing room. His breath left his body and his heart seemed locked in another chest, a strange chest, where it beat instead.

Get away—where did you hear that? Eric said.

Everyone knows it—the birds are singing it. I hear it's a bit of an open marriage there with Jim and her, you know.

I heard—

Ask no questions, that type of thing. She takes this archeologist to a hotel out of town.

John coughed. It echoed around the shelter, a cold being caught and repeated in another throat, and then another, the way things spread. Jim placed a hand on the cubicle wall and lowered himself to the bench and felt the cold stone under his feet, how cold.

Strange enough, Eric said, because I never see Jim with anyone. How long has this been going on?

The word is a couple of years, John said.

Jim took the ends of the towel and placed them over his ears. Archeologist? The wind blew under the cubicle door and up his legs. He felt years blowing in with it, ageing him on the spot. His testicles tightened and the wet hair dripped frigid dots down his neck. Then he heard the whisper of trousers sliding off.

She's a bit of a flirt, all right, Eric said, with the cough that told Jim the trousers were indeed off. Eric always coughed right then.

John said, If I had her body, I'd be a flirt too.

Jim hasn't a clue, does he? I don't think he knows about it at all.

Don't think so—head in the clouds. You've got to like him all the same.

Jim's a decent sort, Eric said. A good man. Always something different.

As he sat, Jim looked around him, looked down at his stomach. Despite months of exercise, the folds of fat were still there. His chest too seemed flabbier, little pouts around his nipples. Another blast of wind shook the door of the cubicle and fried his skin cold into goosebumps. His legs looked thinner, less muscular. The swims had done nothing more than expose how much a body can shrivel, what lay ahead of him. Yes, he was older, as if he had not noticed until his body said, I am fifty-two, and this is you.

His wife was surely happy. Denise and he lived a marriage without questions. His Saturdays were a stroll through the bookshops, a coffee on Shop Street, mingling with the crowd, the smell of fish and pizza on High Street down to the Spanish Arch, and from there a short walk to the swans at the Claddagh. You can judge a marriage by Saturdays, Jim thought. The inside of the shelter darkened. He moved his shoulders, must leave soon. But he did not want to make his friends feel bad.

Eric said, At some stage you have to wonder if Jim can do the business.

Not true at all, John said. Remember Lucy at the department dinner? I heard Jim and she went into the bathroom and she came out fixing her dress. Jim walked out a little later and headed for the bar.

Jim shook his head. He never touched that woman and had gone to the bathroom to escape her. He stood and waved his arms to get warm.

Eric said, Interesting. No one ever told me about that, Jim and Lucy. Is it raining yet?

No. We're okay.

I hate this part, taking off my shirt. Kills me.

In the cubicle, Jim felt colder than the wind. He stepped up onto the seat and did weightlifting movements, bending his knees and bringing his backside down to his heels, and back up again, breathing softly. He leaned to the wall and shivered, one hand on the towel to keep it from falling. He was fine in here as long as he didn't make any noise, as his friends never used the cubicle. They always used the same part of the shelter, with Eric on the inside and John nearest the door, and undressed in the same order: trouser leg, shirtsleeve, that stupid cough, the same breathing, the same little jumps between the cracks on the concrete as they bounded for the water. And since they always faced the wall as they got ready, they wouldn't see him if he put his head over the cubicle door.

Lifting himself on his toes, Jim looked.

As expected, John Berry's black left sock was coming off on schedule. Go on, John. Now the top shirt button, that's it, and use your index and thumb—excellent. And now another little cough as you take it off. Jim placed his right knee against the door hinge and his left foot flat across the bench while holding the towel with his right hand and using two fingers of his left on top of the cubicle wall for balance.

John removed the shirt and coughed. It's lot colder today, that's for sure. The fat around John's waist bobbed as he hung the shirt on the third hook from the left. Jim remembered watching him eat bacon and cabbage at Eric's one night, carefully tearing fat from a glistening rind. John Berry folded his trousers and placed them in the bag, giving them the usual tug to get the wrinkles out.

I don't know. He must know about his wife and the archeologist. I don't see how not. I would, I can tell you. In a second.

Jim tried to list all the archeologists he knew.

Eric said, Maybe it's one of those sham marriages. One of them is gay, but they stay together.

Remember Lucy. Unless he goes both ways. Why, Eric, do you fancy him?

Stop! Eric shouted.

They laughed as Jim froze at the level of his eyes behind the cubicle.

Eric said, How about just you and me do the next wind-surfing trip. I don't know about Jim this time.

Yes, just the two of us. Remember him explaining how the nature spirits live in the west? He sat one night by the Cliffs of Moher and waited for them to come out.

He saw them dancing in the moonlight.

Like this? John Berry raised his left arm and danced in a circle, then pulled his stomach in and stood sideways. He looked himself up and down. I have a question.

Yes?

Do you think I've lost weight?

What? A bit, around the waist, yes.

Are you sure, are you being honest now?

I am, I think, yes.

As far as Jim could tell, John weighed himself every day. He did not need anyone to tell him. From his high perch in the cubicle Jim saw that John had lost some hair at the crown, and the fat around his jaw squeezed out a second chin. His knees swelled with arthritis.

This is the first time Jim's missed a swim, John said. Maybe there's trouble with the wife.

Maybe she's seeing that lecturer fellow at the university again.

Again? It never stopped, John said. They were at it last week, from what I hear, in the college bar, off in a corner.

Eric swung his arms. Poor fellow doesn't know half the things she does behind his back. She even came on to me once.

No, John said.

At the annual department party.

Eric folded his sweater. This was the order: he hooked his thumbs under his loose white oversized underpants, turned to the wall, bent as he lifted his right leg and then the left, put the underpants in his bag, and hoisted up his swimming trunks. Then off with the sweater.

Jim waited long seconds as both men rubbed their hands and paced the shelter. To show himself now would bring confrontation, old denials, new defenses. He swallowed and felt the draught of that November morning sweep along the concrete and swirl about the cubicle, rubbing a dull red blade across his ankles. His left foot slid on the wet seat. As he fell, his right knee scraped the hinges. The only thing was to let go. The seat sprang like a see-saw and slammed against the wall.

Jesus, Eric said.

Jim draped the towel over his head and chest. He opened the door.

From under the towel he saw John Berry's black nylon socks and brown shoes under a tight swimsuit. He always put the socks and shoes back on for the run to the sea.

Ah Jesus, Eric said from the shelter entrance.

What? John said, joining him.

Looks like rain.

John turned, Excuse me, what's the water like today?

The simple disguise of a towel and some distance. Jim revolved his wrist in a so-so fashion, the misery of it. He took the bag and turned back for the cubicle.

Eric said, John, come on, let's do the swim before that cloud comes down on us. Let's run at it today and just dive in.

John Berry and Eric Hartman charged out of the shelter.

They would run to the sea and crouch, blowing into their hands. At the last second before diving in, John removes the shoes and socks. They swing back their arms, bend at the knees, and tip over like milk into tea. They swim once around the tower, bodies static but busy, insects in a toilet bowl.

Inside the cubicle again, Jim grabbed for the plastic grocery bag, his shirt, his trousers, socks, shoes and jacket.

It was true that Denise and he had an arrangement. Their personal life was complicated, but only if viewed from the outside. Passion was something he could live without, and he supposed she felt the same. But if he were ever to meet someone he would tell Denise. While not romantic together anymore, they slept in the same bed, and she hadn't said anything about an archeologist or a lecturer. Or it was all malicious gossip.

She would have said something. Jim stood and tightened his belt over the shirt. Yes, she had come home drunk a few times. Yes, she did appear depressed. He'd asked her if anything was wrong. She said she felt tired. Jim lit some candles and massaged her head. You are very good to me, she said, and touched his hands.

Jim placed the wet gear in the bag and sat again in the cubicle. Something you hear through a stall door, from a chance conversation on the street, a phone quickly put down when you enter a room, something you hear that depresses you for an hour and maybe for the rest of your life. He had minutes to get out before the two returned to the shelter, but Jim could not find the will to move. Instead he saw images of Denise, not with another man, not of her naked body, but of her not telling the truth. He watched her in the kitchen not telling the truth, in the garden not telling the truth, watching television not telling the truth. The images slid back in time, and in a few seconds she was not telling the truth ever, all the way back to when they first met. Even then, when he brought her to a film on a rainy Friday after classes and she was still doing her degree, she was not telling him the truth. His stomach moved and he heaved. He cupped a hand over his mouth and clenched his thighs as another blast of wind scoured the shelter, this time carrying in rain on top.

In the final minute of John Berry and Eric Hartman's morning swim, Jim remembered the day of the midsummer wild swim, when he said those words about it being the best day. He had turned and seen them smiling to each other in the cave of the shelter.

Well, why not, he called. Why can't today be the best day?

You might be right, John's shadow said back to him, but I wouldn't bet on it. Not today.

Now it was too late to leave the cubicle. Jim sat until he heard both men enter the shelter in a swish of feet and shivering.

Very cold today, John. Jim missed it.

He's probably out looking for his wife.

Jim grabbed the inside bolt and burst out of the cubicle, a blur of hair and glasses and a shout. Don't you two have anything better to do?

Eric said, Jim.

Is this what goes on behind my back?

John took a towel. No, Jim.

Eric said, Was that you earlier?

Yes, I heard it all, Jim said.

Fun, that's all it was.

Jim said, Eric, you can't keep your mouth shut, that's why no one tells you anything, nobody except this fellow here. He pointed at John, And your wife wants to leave you.

Now look, John said.

Jim said, And ask me how I know that.

She doesn't want to leave me.

Because she told me. She told me months ago when I was picking you up that day your car was in for service.

John shook his head, looked at the ground.

Jim said, All those pills. He walked to the door of the shelter. The rain was picking up, and he felt it swamp his shoulders.

You'd better leave, Eric said. You're saying foolish things.

John took a step. Leave, Jim. We know you're upset.

You know nothing about me. Don't talk to me again, either of you.

Jim walked the promenade to his car, started the engine and turned the heater up to a blast. Over Galway Bay, the heavy cloud combed the water into fluff and rocked the car with a gust that spattered drops on the left window. He watched Hartman and Berry run from the shelter with their bags. He felt fists rummage in his kidneys.

He knew, yes, he did, but he loved her too much to say anything. And she had been kind to him the morning of the strange and dangerous swim when he got home and could not wait to tell her about it, since they did not have such moments any more, he and Denise, when he could tell her something new. She said he was foolish to try that, but she laughed too and smiled at him, a smile he knew from a long time before. And he thought briefly that there might be hope.

On the promenade through the downpour he saw his friends raise a hand to each other and shrink to unlock their doors. John Berry dragged his jacket over his head. Jim sat with his hands on the steering wheel, waiting for the car to warm up. The shower stretched the bodies of his friends across the glass, melted them down the windshield, and finally made them strangers.

HOW LONG UNTIL

AFEW MINUTES OUT OF DUBLIN while driving west on the road to Galway, Peter asked his wife, If I died tomorrow, how long would you wait until you did it with someone else?

He accelerated past a slow-moving car as Brenda stared: Before I did *what*?

You know, slept with someone else. How long would you wait if I died tomorrow?

She looked him up and down. That's a terrible question. Jesus, what made you think of that? She fixed her sunglasses against the evening glare and crossed her arms.

So no answer then, Peter said.

They passed under the bridge at Maynooth and slowed into heavy traffic. A bank-holiday weekend in June and everyone was heading west it seemed. Peter lowered the flap to get the sun out of his eyes. He wanted to tell her that he'd just seen a hoarding for life insurance and that he'd thought about what would happen if he were killed and she was alone. Of course that got him thinking about how long she'd wait until being with another man. The image of her making love with someone now a stranger to her had stung him, and then he reasoned that maybe she already knew the man; maybe his replacement was at that moment drinking a cup of coffee or jogging or watching television somewhere within a few miles of them, that man. The compulsion to ask was upon him, and without waiting, he had asked.

Brenda said nothing more and kept her arms crossed.

So much for counting to ten before opening your mouth. He didn't want her to know that a roadside advertisement spurred him to ask such a foolish question, so he said nothing too and braked his way forward, tapping the steering wheel to the radio until they approached the same advertisement a mile down the road.

A rough guess then, he said.

She turned like a loose spring. Look, I'm not going to answer you. Are you thinking about doing something?

No, no. I just wanted to know. It was a question, that's all. He moved his arms to support his innocence and felt the first twinge of regret. Now he wanted to forget the whole thing, but the question wasn't finished with him yet: he saw it move up closer, intent on staying in the rear-view mirror. The cars moved in small jerks. In a few miles surely it would open up. The steering wheel felt clammy in his hands, but he thought how her jealousy pleased him, if that's what it was. He wanted to lower the window, but Brenda hated the exhaust fumes and the air conditioner didn't work well unless the car was moving. The sun dipped into his eyes and the visor wouldn't go low enough. He leaned back in the seat and stretched, felt tired.

They were driving to Galway to spend the weekend with Brenda's parents. She was upset and the trip would be murder now, he already heard it coming at him with its knives, sharpening the Saturday across the Sunday.

Ten minutes later she spoke again: Killed suddenly or died slowly?

He answered without thinking because he wanted to get rid of the entire conversation, let it unravel and die.

What does it matter?

Well if you were killed in an accident, I'd be in shock and I don't think I'd want to be with anyone for a long time. But if you died slowly, in a hospital bed, something like a terminal illness, that would be different, I suppose.

She uncrossed her arms now and appeared to relax again, but Peter felt he had to continue it now.

Very well. I die from an illness. How different is that?

She said, In that case I'd probably wait, I don't know, three months.

Peter felt his heart bounce. What was that? Three months? You'd wait twelve Saturdays? For the love of—

No need to be so upset because it's just a guess.

He moved into the left lane to avoid the accident that must have caused the hold-up. So did twenty others, jerky, fidgety types rammed up against each other, prizing out inches by the brake. The stopping and starting made him carsick, something he'd had since a child. He recalculated the weeks out of the months just to make sure he got it right.

Twelve Saturdays, he said.

You asked, she said.

Oh come on, he muttered. The car ahead blocked him and someone else darted into the lane.

I hope you're not going to be in a mood all evening

because I just answered your question, she said, because that's all I did, you know, answer—

I know.

—your question.

He thought of that invisible man tugging off her blouse and then couldn't bring the thought to a stop. The stupid thing was that they were both in their early thirties so they didn't even need to be thinking about these things, and now everything was spinning like a coin, a question he'd flipped into the air inspired by that life-insurance advertisement he saw with a fat actor on it who looked like he had a day to live and who was probably at that moment swilling beer in his living room and punching channels out of the remote, doubtlessly unaware of the chain of events he had set in motion with those big black letters over his head, the ones Peter read thirty minutes ago as they drove along the congested road: What would your loved ones do if you died tomorrow?

When they reached Athlone an hour later Peter said he wanted to sit in the cool roadside café and maybe have a coffee and wake up, but she said she wanted to keep going, that they were past halfway. The plan was to stay in a hotel in Galway, something he said would be the right thing to do since they didn't want her parents waiting up for them. The real reason was that it was one night less with two people he'd never really liked and who didn't like him. Not quite good enough for their only daughter. They had retired to Galway a few years before, bought in before the prices took off.

As they sped on the motorway, Brenda turned to him. The road narrowed back to a two-way system and to the words she spoke, the slightly sad eyes that contradicted her smile.

I've thought about doing it when you've been away on buying trips.

He weaned the car in behind a large bus on the winding, narrow road. Couldn't see a thing, couldn't overtake for miles now. All these cars, nowhere to go. Then what she'd said overtook him and he replayed it and suddenly couldn't look at her. He had asked the question, asked for this, and got his answer and everything that was to come.

I've thought about it, she said.

The bus belched exhaust and the car behind was flashing him to speed up.

He said, Fair enough. That's why I asked in the first place. I just wanted to know how long you'd wait, that was all.

Brenda said, And don't tell me you haven't looked at women and wanted to. I've watched you look at them when we go out together.

What she said was true. He'd seen women in bars and on the street and if they'd pursued him he might have gone along with it. He wanted to admit that now but was afraid what she'd think if he did. The sun sank to the tops of the trees, brushing red along the sky, sketching the night.

I've never slept with anyone since we married, if that's what you mean, he said, desperate for her to repeat it back.

So, she said. I'm supposed to say the same to you now. You bring this up at the beginning of our trip to my parents' house and I don't know why.

Neither do I. He turned the tuning dial from a weak station. I'm sorry, Brenda.

He leaned into the steering wheel. Better never to have said anything, to have let it go and thought about it instead at three in the morning like everyone else, about companionship. The fellow on the insurance sign was most likely settling into this Friday evening of the long weekend, loosening his belt.

An hour later they reached the outskirts of Galway; it was fully night and headlights laced the road like beads on a necklace. Brenda pointed off the road: Here, Peter, I think this is our hotel. As he made the turn she said, You know, being with someone is sometimes about having a friend, a companion.

Sensing a thaw, Peter said, I swear to you that I was thinking the exact same thing about companionship when we were going past Athlone.

She smiled. But you didn't say anything, Peter. I wish you'd be more spontaneous.

He took a side road. You mean impulsive?

That's not what I said. I said *spontaneous*. You have to live life, right?

As they drove to the hotel, he chewed over her last sentence. Four years married and both working with their own careers, doing well, money in the bank, shopping trips to New York. He'd often thought about leaving her, nothing he ever said to his friends. Didn't know why. It came to him when the sunlight hit the trees at a certain angle: life in a different place. If he acted on that impulse, scraped the hesitation off and lived life that way, their marriage was over. Then he wondered what kept any couple together, what preserved a marriage from the people in it.

Her voice had changed recently, though he couldn't put an exact date on it. Her tone always softened when she called him at work, and that was the only way he knew she was addressing him and not someone sitting next to her at the reception counter where she worked. She had a habit of talking to other people at the same time without any transition, so he often answered a question she had asked someone else and was still answering when she came back to him.

How to know if a woman is leaving you, that's the major question for the man who wants this kind of insurance. He counted the ways: I'm going to a golf outing, it's for work. I should be back tomorrow. More ominous: I need to plan our weekends in advance because I have some clients to meet. The end is very close when you hear, My work is really important to me.

His heart raced and his breath pooled in his chest as he pictured webs of deceit spun around her. The reason he came up with those examples was that she had said all of those things lately. He transported every imaginary word to its real meaning: I'm going to the shop. Translation: I want some privacy so I can phone my new friend. I'm going for a few drinks after work. Translation: We're driving to his place.

Peter sighed the insanity out of himself. This kind of thinking was destructive. Maybe it was Dublin, the city had been getting to him. He pulled into a parking space and glanced out the window: the hotel, a restaurant, petrol stations in a strip, the rest was night.

This place, he thought, could be marked as loneliness on a map. Galway had spread in the past decade, gushing for miles along the roads that led to it, pink and blue neon signs, huge hotels standing alone till more business built up around them, and then the rabbit-cage houses. But he knew that Brenda saw a different Galway, the one she grew up in, and how important this trip was. She worked hard and didn't get much time off anymore. He wanted to clear up the stupid misunderstanding that threatened to veer out of control, to undo that strange risk he took instead of playing it safe and small-talking away the trip, which is what he clearly ought to have done instead, the same way insured people talk.

But that's not what he did, and suddenly he needed to know everything. As they got out of the car, he spoke over the roof: I want to know if you've been with anyone else since we got married.

It's something I think about, just like you do.

Who have you thought of doing it with? Anyone I know?

Almost everyone you know, Peter.

He shivered, dressed only in a shirt. Maybe it was the night; even in June, the nights were cold.

What, Brenda? Have you slept with anyone?

You first. Have you been with anyone else since we met?

No, he said.

Then I can say no.

What do you mean, you can say no?

I haven't slept with anyone, she said.

We're speaking the truth here? We're happy, aren't we?

I'm tired, Peter.

He shook his head. A sign leads to divorce. He'd be alone again.

Loneliness started when his mother once left him alone

in a supermarket to get something. I'll be back in a minute, Peter. Even though he didn't move a single step, his mother didn't come back for him. He waited and then he waited. Then he went looking for her. A man asked him if he needed help. When Peter began to run, the man walked faster, his two steps for Peter's four. Peter shouted again and again until his mother shook him quiet, telling him she'd only been gone three minutes.

Peter turned to Brenda as they walked into the hotel. Let me understand this. I look at other women, but you haven't slept with anyone.

She stopped and they stood facing each other in the foyer.

To be honest?

Yes, honest.

I'd like a man who doesn't always wash his hair or shave, she said. You know?

Peter nodded. She was critiquing him. His job required that he present a neat appearance at all times, and he'd gotten into the habit of being that way all the time.

I know the type, he said. One who doesn't have a job.

As if he had said nothing, she continued, I'd like a man who doesn't always treat me so well, be so nice at all times. I don't know, Peter. But intelligent too.

A little bit of everything, then.

Don't be sarcastic. It's not you.

The receptionist looked up. Peter didn't care.

It's not every man who gets to talk about these things with his wife.

She laughed. And who started this? Anyway, what type would you replace *me* with?

Someone like you, he said.

I don't think so, Peter. I think you want someone—she paused—a lot safer, maybe more sophisticated than me. She winked. I'm a little too much for you, aren't I?

Maybe, maybe not.

I'm hungry, she said.

She walked to the counter, stood as far from him as she could take herself, silent behind her sunglasses in the dark, with her arms crossed again, and as the weight of that question pressed harder on him than ever, he fumed at Brenda and at himself. Like the signs strung along the road from Dublin for insurance and banking and hotels and holidays, like the plot of a slow film, that simple question, the one he'd asked without much thought, still ran in his mind, changing from 'How long would you wait until,' to 'Peter, why did you have to ask that question,' to the shout, What were you thinking when you asked that question?

They walked to the elevator. Maybe because Brenda was better at silence than he was, he spoke the next words that came into his head, again without thinking too much first.

What if we came to an arrangement?

She looked at him. What kind of arrangement?

You could see others, as long as I knew—

Knew?

Or maybe, I don't mean actually—

You want me to see other men? The sunglasses were off.

I want you to do whatever you want, because you will anyway. I know you.

I wonder, Peter, if you know me.

All you have to do is tell me. It'll be okay, I promise.

Her tone changed again, this time flat, more friendly.

You really mean that?

He nodded. So she was interested. An arrangement would be arrived at, mutually satisfying, or mutually unsatisfying, but at least he was insured against surprises that way. No friends telling him they'd seen Brenda having a candlelit dinner with someone in a restaurant.

Before or after, she said.

I wouldn't mind, if we were at a party and you met someone. We could go into a room or you could take him to a hotel and I could wait in the car or, he opened his palm, you could call me and say, 'Peter, I've just been with someone.'

Brenda shook her head, put a hand up to her forehead. He felt he was doing well, speaking his mind again, no filter, no hesitation, no figuring out the right phrase first. This was healthy.

Or is that too much for you? he said.

Damn you, she whispered, and stormed out of the elevator and went the wrong way, had to come back when he was already in the room. She didn't put her bag on the floor, just stood in the doorway.

I'm going to my parents' place, she said. I'll be back later.

She left with the car keys. He showered and dried himself as he stood naked in front of the window. He was sure no one could see him. He watched a short blonde walk to her car. He dressed and went downstairs to the lobby, hungry now.

The person at the registration counter scribbled loudly while speaking into the soft buzz of a phone. Fish swam in the aquarium. Two women drifted in from the street and walked to the adjacent bar. Peter watched them. One caught his eye and smiled. The man on the insurance hoarding was probably asleep now, dreaming, a happy drunk because he was insured. Peter wanted to be safe now more than he wanted all the women in the world, real or imagined. He wanted to be the man on the sign. Good things happened to safe people. They could wait out the nonsense, be smug and just wait.

The waiter moved at Peter's shoulder, and as he sipped the coffee he thought Brenda might be teasing him about being spontaneous. Maybe she meant swinging with other couples, because she was wild in bed sometimes, though lately not much. Maybe she was meeting strangers in strange rooms already: Dublin had its fair share of swingers, it was an active lifestyle, he'd seen the ads, heard friends mention it in passing. Maybe they were missing out on the whole thing.

After he went back upstairs he pulled the orange blinds, took up the remote and flipped through the channels. He checked the pay-per-view listings and punched in the codes for a porn film. He turned up the volume, took off his shoes and trousers and lay back on the bed. The opening shots showed flashes of threesomes and women sitting in armchairs holding toys and looking straight at the camera saying, I'm waiting for you.

The telephone call was expensive, and in a hotel, astronomical. Peter added up the time in his mind and figured that a call would cost him less if they got straight down to it and avoided introductions, which he knew wouldn't happen because they were there to make money and he'd find it hard to hang up once he made any kind of a connection, even anonymously. He'd talk long-winded nonsense just to be polite and end up with a gigantic bill from some outfit called Excelsior Communications on his credit card. The feature began. An actress kissed a man. Peter liked her hair and thought of Brenda. The blonde actress sat on the man, rubbed herself, squeezed her thighs. Peter shut his eyes tight, and as he turned Brenda over and over in his fantasy, she called out his name, her voice strangely under control, even cold, it seemed to him.

Peter.

He kept his eyes closed.

I'm here.

He looked. Brenda stood by the bed, arms folded. What are you doing, she said.

They both watched the screen where a naked woman brushed a man's nipples with her hair. Peter looked from the movie to Brenda. She lit a cigarette and stared at the wall. Cries of passion mixed with the background elevator music.

I suppose this is acting on your impulses, she said.

In the bathroom Peter washed his hands and splashed water on his face. When he looked up, he saw Brenda in the bathroom mirror. Behind her, the angled television images flashed in the dark hotel room.

She drew the blinds and they slept.

In the morning she didn't want any breakfast, and they rejoined the Saturday traffic in silence, crossing the city and driving a few miles towards Barna. They moved in and out of the ocean views. Shortly after ten in the morning they parked on a tree-lined street and Brenda went straight in, and after he followed and after the greetings, she climbed the stairs. Her mother—Bernadette—went after her, and then a door closed on the landing.

Peter sat at the coffee table and chatted with the husband, Sean, whose eyes kept darting from him to something over his shoulder. Peter finally turned and looked out the window, saw a few brown leaves skid across the grass of the garden. Sean made an awkward gesture when his wife called to him from upstairs. He said, Excuse me, Peter.

When they all came back down, Sean walked out to the garden and the mother directed Peter like an orchestra of one. This chair, Peter. This cup's for you, Peter. That's why he couldn't stand them. Smug people, ordering him around with a smile, their territory, all those little victories.

I'll check the bacon, Brenda said. She held a glass of red wine. After a couple of glasses, she always got a bit down. Red wine at night, husband's delight. Red wine in the morning, husband's warning.

And hasn't this been the strangest beginning to a summer you've ever seen, Bernadette said, fingering her china. Cloudy and even cold in the evenings, and the leaves are everywhere still.

Peter watched through the window as Sean chased a leaf and put it in a plastic bag.

He said, I like it, I like the cold.

Oh, Peter, wait a few years until you're my age. She glanced at her husband outside. You won't like the cold then.

Outside, Sean shook off his shoes at the door and shuffled back to his seat. Damned cold out there. And those leaves.

Now, Sean, you can't control the neighbor's tree,

Bernadette said. Every year, it's the same. Leaves in twos and threes all the way through spring, but Sean catches them all in the end.

Peter, there's talk of prices stagnating in the property market, temporarily, I'm sure of it, Sean said. Will you be staying in Dublin?

I'm sure Peter doesn't want to be discussing that so soon after arriving, Bernadette said, pouring a cup.

Peter shifted. The curtains were open and the sun had somehow found him again. Damn thing following him everywhere. Light hurt his eyes and made his nose water. He squeezed his eyes, pinched the bridge of his nose and breathed deep. The wind plastered a leaf to the glass. He did not want to open his eyes and see Sean glare at the leaf. He did not want to open his eyes at all. The clink of china tapped at his eardrum.

Now, Peter, how is business? Have you been promoted? Bernadette said.

He shook his head. Where's Brenda? Is she still upstairs?

She's in the kitchen, she said. Didn't you see her go in?

He walked to the kitchen door and saw his wife leaning over the sink. Her finger underlined her nose, and she appeared to be crying. A drop reached the end of her finger and swung loose like string.

I didn't see you come in here, he said.

She shook her head and kept her back to him as she reached for the freezer door. He watched, unable to leave or stay. He had made a terrible mistake.

Brenda, I'm sorry I asked that question. I don't think you've ever done anything.

She spooned the ice cream into a bowl and lifted the

wine glass. As he waited for her to say something, anything, he heard her mother in the living room.

Sean, there's another leaf, Sean.

And as he waited longer, he wondered if at a certain age women ran out of forgiveness.

It was just a question, he said.

SHOPLIFTING IN THE USA

BOB, THE SUPERMARKET OWNER, was adamant this time. I noticed him gesturing to me from the end of the aisle I was restocking with tinned beans, but I pretended not to see him. Then he hissed, and when I looked up, he put a finger to his lips. In the stock room he leaned over the security camera, shielding his eyes from the fluorescent lights.

What is it, Bob? I said.

Look. He pointed at a blurred image.

I took off my apron and lifted the peak of my cap. I could see the whole supermarket divided between the security cameras. Fifteen, twenty customers, three cashiers, one of them filing her nails, another flipping through a magazine.

I can see the aisles, I said. Is that what you want me to see?

Look! Bob pressed a fingertip into the belly of a stocky teenager—eighteen, nineteen—who was standing in the third aisle with his hands in his pockets.

I see him, I said.

The teenager moved to the left of Bob's finger and picked up a jar, glanced left and right, and slipped it under his jacket.

Now I've got you, Bob said.

What else has he taken?

Three or four packets of something, I think. I'll get him before he leaves.

You can't. He has to leave the premises first. We've been through this before. I'll call the police.

Bob pointed at the screen and shouted. The police? He's stealing that food out of my children's mouths. He'll be long gone.

He grabbed a stick from the corner and took a practice swing. Then the minute he steps outside, he said, his glasses stained with sweat.

You'll get sued for every penny you have, I said.

I don't care. What's he doing now?

We leaned over the monitor, our noses almost touching. I saw the boy freeze in the aisle. He was looking into the air around him, must have heard the shouting but couldn't see anybody. We could see him thinking. Then he looked straight at the camera.

Too late. He knows, I said.

The shoplifter opened his jacket and put the packets back on the shelf, then piece by piece all the other stuff, including items we hadn't seen from his pockets. Once the returns were completed, he zipped up and patted his pockets as if to check for anything he might have forgotten.

He's put everything back, I said. We can't do a thing.

Bob let a grunt out in degrees as his eyes bored into the video screen while the boy moved through the cashier station, checked his watch, looked around him and grabbed a carton of cigarettes before dashing out.

I turned to hold Bob but he eluded me easily for a big guy. I raced outside after him and saw him catch up with the shoplifter down the street, swinging at him in front of everyone, missing with every shot. The teenager twisted like a kite, laughing. I got between them and took a hit in the back and yelled. Bob pushed me aside.

For a few seconds everyone froze. The shoplifter hesitated. You could see him considering the possibilities: lawsuit, emotional this, disability that. But he'd have to call the police first, and that was not an option for this fellow apparently.

So instead he slammed a fist into Bob's nose. When Bob caught hold of his wrist, the thief knocked Bob's glasses off and poked at his eyeball with the other, then skipped off and wove through the traffic.

Bob walked in a circle, not knowing what to grope for, his glasses swinging from one ear.

Show's over, I said to the crowd. Someone laughed, someone cheered. I picked up the carton and helped Bob back to the supermarket stock room.

You should have waited for the authorities, I said.

Later, at home, I told Heather about Bob and the kid while I poured myself a cup of tea.

That means Julia will be calling any minute to report that Bob is sulking, she said.

I sipped at the tea. The phone rang. Heather picked it up and nodded.

Yes, Julia. I know. He just loses himself completely.

I envisioned Bob sitting in front of the television in his old armchair, rocking with his eyeballs fixed straight ahead at the wall. We all knew he had a bad temper, and the people around him softened it, but one day the temper would find him all alone.

I can't believe he swung at that shoplifter, I said to Heather after she put the phone down.

Yes, even after the boy put most of the things back, she said.

I smiled and remembered I'd married Heather because she saw the world in a simpler way than I did. She was American, and we'd lived there for thirteen years before I told her I wanted to move back to Ireland. Bob was from Texas, and in the late eighties he bought a small supermarket in Ennis where three roads crossed on the way to the airport: a lot of business from lost drivers buying a snack to ask a question. After I arrived back in Ireland with Heather he gave me a job, even with my history.

What surprises me, I said, is that Bob followed through on what he said. He's always saying what he'll do and then pretends he's done it. I caught him lying once.

Wait, I'm getting an ice cream, I want to hear it all. Heather went out to the kitchen.

Well, I said, we had a customer a while back who wrote a few bad checks in the space of a week. Bob told me he traced the address and then confronted the customer on the street, pushed him against the wall and asked him if he'd like to rob him now. To go ahead and rob him now. Bob had me convinced he'd actually done it.

So how do you know he was lying?

The same man came into the supermarket that day and wrote another check. Not a mark on him.

She said, That's strange behavior.

She sat back in her armchair and blew smoke. I hope Bob isn't too angry, she said.

What do you mean? I said.

I'm asking him for a job, that's what I mean. I need to buy a treadmill—look at me, I'm sixty pounds overweight, the doctor told me.

I walked in a circle before saying anything. Heather, we talked about this before. We can't both work at the super-market.

But I'll work evenings.

I couldn't believe it, Heather wanting to work with Bob. We'd never see each other except at night. I'd heard what happened to couples who did that, and it was either all good or all bad. But I knew that once Heather fixed something in her mind, she'd follow it through. I also thought about what to do once I got my college degree, and whether she would go along with whatever that plan might be. It occurred to me that we had some changes coming up. I was tired of the same job, the same voices.

She did her first day at the supermarket the following week. We passed each other at the entrance. She wore an embroidered jacket, tracksuit bottoms and tennis shoes, a dress-code violation.

That's a great start, I said.

Don't you dare criticize me, she said.

Two days passed. At six in the evening the phone rang at home. It was Bob.

I need to talk to you, he said.

Okay, talk to me.

It's private. Tomorrow. He hung up.

In the morning after I clocked in, I went straight to the stock room. He was there, swaying back and forth on the balls of his feet, waiting for me. He clicked the play button on the video player.

Watch the tape, he said.

I stood in front of the monitor and watched people shopping for five minutes.

Bob, what do you want me to see?

Watch the tape. I rewound it so you won't miss anything.

The tape showed the supermarket emptying. Camera switches to Heather at the cash register, looking around her. Heather walking into the aisles. Heather ambling into the left-hand corner of another screen, lifting a bag of crisps, wedging it inside her jacket.

I closed my eyes.

Bob waved his finger at me. The Bible says that what you take gets multiplied a hundredfold in things taken from you.

The Bible doesn't say that, I said. What you give is given you a hundredfold.

Same thing, except in reverse, he said.

I'll pay for them.

Bob shook his head, the face of a dragonfly.

What can I do then? I said.

He said, Get back to work.

Heather was nonchalant when I confronted her at home. It was just a bag of crisps, she said.

I told you about the cameras, didn't I?

I forgot. I was hungry.

The following morning I left a note on Bob's desk offering him ten times what the crisps were worth.

He came up to me in the supermarket that morning with a receipt he picked off the aisle floor. On the back was NO in big letters. We passed the day in silence. I was worried about his apparent calm. I preferred him when he was ranting.

Heather and I didn't sleep well for a few nights, so I decided to resolve the issue once and for all. Without telling her, I asked Bob to join me for a drink after work. He met me at my usual table outside and acted friendly, knocking the drinks back and telling me jokes as if nothing was going on between us. I waited, caught the first silence, and put my Guinness down.

Bob, I said, we've known each other for about ten years.

Yes, he said.

And we all have our idiosyncrasies. It was a word I'd found in the thesaurus. Bob looked puzzled.

I said, We act different from one another.

Where's this going, he said, looking nervous.

I don't know where it's going, Bob. That's the whole point. This pretending you do.

What pretending?

You invent bad things you've done, and now you've got me worried about my wife and the bag of crisps.

What have I invented?

You made up what you did to the man who wrote the bad checks. He came in the same day. Were the checks even bad?

Bob swallowed. That was a practice run. I was working out a plan of action in my head, you know, out loud.

Do you really expect me to believe that? You never touched him then or later, did you?

He shouted, He was a good customer, I just told you that. I was practicing in my head for the bad ones.

I took a sip to let him calm down.

For your information, he said, look at what I did to that shoplifter. You saw me. That's what you get if you shoplift in the USA.

He made swinging motions with his arms.

Stop it, Bob. I never saw you like this until a few months ago. What's wrong with you?

What are you doing? he shouted, standing beside me. I could smell the aftershave even that late in the day. People were watching us.

What do you mean, What am I doing?

For the rest of your life? What are you doing? He broke a big sweat, fixed me with a pebbly eye.

I said, You've lost me.

John, I've got that supermarket, and that's it. I don't have any talent for anything. I was born for that place. I had it written on my forehead when I was fifteen. All my money and one suitcase is in that place. But you've got that librarian, the one I hired part-time, talking about you at the checkout, how you read all these books, that you're thinking of doing a degree at the technical college. Don't you think I know all about that?

Oh, come on, I just mentioned it to her one day when the shop was empty.

And that's fine that you're smart, John. But I've got nothing except my business, and when people rob me, it's personal.

It was a bag of crisps, for the love of God.

I felt sorry for him right then because he was as real as he would ever get. I reached for my drink instead of his neck. He rolled a cigarette in the scissors of his fingers.

You can afford to be relaxed about it, because your future is secure, Bob said.

Which future are we talking about?

You'll get a better job with that degree and leave.

I just mentioned it, Bob, I'm not enrolled anywhere. I don't even have enough money for college yet.

Yet? Bob said. I knew it.

My future isn't secure, Bob, and neither is yours.

I won't fire you.

No, I mean that chain supermarket from England opening soon down the street. They'll undercut you the way you did the smaller shops.

I'll keep my prices low, he said, his voice a dogfight.

That's good, I said. But most people I know are living from payday to payday.

He nodded. I sensed an opening.

So why are you so upset about Heather and the crisps?

Bob smiled and tightened one end of the cigarette he wasn't allowed light in the pub. He coughed and brushed the end of his nose, then leaned forward and motioned me to him. We were nose to nose.

Because I don't like her, he said.

I did not move away. What he said was a little like a piece of glue that held me to him. He was telling the truth, the way he said it to me softly, not that crazy rant.

You don't like her?

No. He shook his head and smiled again. But she can work at the store as long as she wants.

That night in bed I snaked my arm under Heather's head and watched the ceiling fan turn above us. I told her that Bob and I had settled the problem.

I felt her voice vibrate before her words came together:

I don't care what you say. The man's got a bad streak in him. He's dangerous, she said.

Then don't steal anything, I said.

She lay on an elbow and whispered, I think I've been stealing for most of my life.

It generally takes a man until he's forty to learn to keep his mouth shut at times like this. So I took a few breaths and said nothing.

Yes, she said. Started when I was six or seven. Some chocolate from the supermarket. I got a big thrill out of it. Went back, always something different. Went on like that for years, small items, food mostly.

I suppose a lot of young people do that at some stage, I said.

She laid her head on my arm and pulled the sheets up to her chin.

Then as I got older, I stole bigger things.

Oh? Like what? Her head felt heavier.

Oh, some tools from the neighbours' sheds. Wrenches, hammers, that kind of thing.

I pictured her stealing from people's sheds. What did you do with them?

I don't know—threw them away, I think. I watched them searching on the weekends, arguing about who left what where.

Heather, I laughed. That was a bit mean.

She shifted in the bed. When I got bigger, I went farther down the street and took money from people's houses, from parked cars. I took purses, rings, photographs.

Sweat ran off her neck and warmed my arm. My heart must have felt her closer to it, the way it was beating now.

You didn't get caught?

She shook her head. No one gave me a second look. That happens when you're plain, like me.

Who said anything about plain? I wanted to sit up, but her head had my arm pinned and her words droned along it to me like a tiny engine.

And one day I stole a child's tricycle from a few doors down, just after Christmas. I watched the parents looking for it.

Wait a minute—you took it from your own street?

Yes. I gave it to my sister's boy as a present.

But she lives only three miles from where you lived. The child must have seen it.

That's rubbish, she said. She reached for her magazine. The pins and needles flooded my arm and I moved it from anywhere she might rest her head again.

What if they drove around, saw your sister's boy riding it?

She licked her thumb and stopped at a photograph. They never found it.

Heather's body coated my left side with damp. She turned to me.

My best ever was stealing a computer from a bedroom. I did that in my final year at school. She was a girl who studied all the time.

From her bedroom?

And all the disks too, even the ones she put away in her drawer.

My heart was doing a quick jog now. Did you sell the computer then?

Her head moved from side to side. No, I drove a few miles outside town and dumped it by the roadside.

Somehow she'd found my arm again and I tried to pull it away.

I said, Heather, this is surprising and upsetting.

Why, John?

You could have gotten caught. You always get caught in the end. Nothing but trouble, stealing.

Really, John?

I looked away, and the only thing I could find to stare at was the window, which was closed.

Heather looked at me. Anyway, finally I stole you. Remember your girlfriend Cynthia?

Cynthia was my fiancée before she ended things out of the blue and left for Europe. No number, no address. Took me a year and some months to get over her. I was shy to begin with and had invested all of my hope in her. And then she disappeared. I went to pieces in front of everyone, dropped out of college, drank heavily, broke into a house, broke into a few houses, was caught and spent four months in jail. You don't think about cameras when you're drunk. Bob was the only one who offered me a start after that, when I was back in Ireland, penniless in my own country with my American wife.

I told her you had a disease, Heather said.

You told Cynthia—a disease?

I can't remember which one, it's been so long. I think I might have said venereal or a low white blood-cell count. Anyway, something not good.

My arm lost the rest of its blood, I was sure of it, under Heather's head.

Why?

Then I made sure I went to all the pubs you went to so

that I would be there to comfort you when you got drunk and depressed.

Heather, I asked you why.

I followed you when you went shopping, so we'd bump into each other and I could ask you how you were doing.

I freed my arm by pulling it out from under her.

She continued, Then you went to jail, and after you got out, then I happened to be going to the same cinema you were, and we sat together, and I held your arm one night during a horror film.

That made sense because I remembered watching only horror at that time. Heather wasn't finished.

I lost weight, had a new hairdo, got nice and tanned for you.

I can't believe this.

Believe it. I wanted you, she said. I was entitled.

I threw back the covers and got out of bed, looking down at her.

She smiled, And now I have you, and it all worked out anyway, and that's why I'm telling you.

Until I breathed in the full cold of the silence that followed, I did not know how simple *simple* was for Heather.

I stared as I spoke, So you think Bob is dangerous?

She turned over and pulled the covers to her side. I stood because that was my only option until I came up with something better. The world might be full of danger, but that's not what brings you down in the end. The man— the philosopher in France—wrote, Hell is other people. I wanted it to be true that people like me can survive, but hope can break if you keep insisting on telling yourself the truth.

I turned out the light. Now here was the obvious: Heather had stolen my life. But I needed to go to the bathroom. So I switched on the light and stood over the bowl. Nothing came. I flushed the toilet anyway, went back and lay as far from her on the bed as I could manage and not fall off.

Heather said, Did you remember to set the alarm?

Yes.

Okay. Goodnight then.

I waited for the rage. But the hour was late and I was tired.

Goodnight, John, she said.

A breeze lifted the curtains and the cold air grazed my shoulder. I pulled the covers over me. She tugged back, using her shoulder as a wedge, and the blanket stretched like a sail between us.

COUNTRY OF THE GRAND

A S HE LEFT THE HOUSE that morning, Frank Delaney remembered being so young that he was not able to walk, struggling from his father to his mother, going soft at the knees and collapsing into her hands. This was the image that reached for him across almost fifty years as he stood at the door and snapped his briefcase shut. It promised to be a busy day at the office, and this was the image that accompanied him down the hallway.

His wife called from the kitchen: Don't forget the dinner party, I'm having friends over.

Their son, who slouched in the hall with his university books, said that he could not be back in time, something about meeting friends in town and being late. Frank said one goodbye to them both and walked out to the car.

The Galway traffic was stop and start. He listened to the news and pulled carefully on a cigarette, made three right turns and reached the bridge that on any other day he would have crossed on his way to work, but the childhood memory made him think of the house he lived in as a teenager, and the impulse to see it again meant that he now turned left at the bridge instead of going straight. Though the house was only three miles away across town, he hadn't seen it in a decade and always assumed it remained more or less the same.

He drove slowly up the hill and waited at a crossroads traffic light. Already he could see that the street had been widened, and when he stopped outside the low white wall of Number 5, he saw that the tree that used to be in the front garden was gone, along with the white and red geraniums he planted thirty-two years ago. The lawn was a concrete parking space with three cars angled into it. As for the house itself, an extension made the front unrecognizable except for the number on the door. His mother used to sit in that glass porch waiting for a conversation or asleep with the newspaper spread on her lap.

Frank bent low in the seat and looked at the upstairs windows, seeing the boy who used to sleep inside those windows. He looked right and left for his childhood friends, the boy with the clubbed foot who tried to keep up with the football game and ran in circles after nothing, the brown sausage dog Rolo who bolted out of a side alley when he heard anyone pass.

The front door of the house opened and two girls, one in a red dress, the other in yellow, walked to the cars. Hidden behind them was the kitchen he ate breakfasts in, the living room where he watched the television with his father by the evening turf fire as the sun set in the familiar folds of the lace curtains. He thought that he should walk up and tell those girls he lived here once, ask to go inside for a second. He said this to himself and then drove off to his office downtown.

Frank worked as a solicitor, and Friday was a day for reviewing the week's litigation and planning next week's. As a senior member of the firm, his office had a rare view of the courtyard fountain. Some of the junior solicitors, whose view was the pictures they put on their cramped walls, brought letters and contracts to him every Friday for review, and he read each word and checked every punctuation mark, since a wrong comma can change the direction of a sentence and lose a case.

During the tea break his mobile phone vibrated into a light on the screen: a message icon and his wife's business number. He put the phone into his pocket without going to voicemail. A knock on the door became a young face, a recent hire.

Yes, what is it?

It's Mr. O'Toole. The matter of the noise after dark. He's tried in good faith to—

Frank nodded through the next ten seconds, noisy students living next door to a settled resident. An old story. The boy finished and stood with his hand on the door.

Frank said, Ask Mr. O'Toole if he wishes to proceed with a suit against the owner of the rented house.

He brought his tea to the window: the saplings in their large pots made a square in the concrete yard and doubtless thrived from the fountain spray. Between the rooftops the Salmon river emptied into Galway Bay. This scene was a balm after the upset of what he saw on his old street. Yes, everything familiar for a change.

The morning passed in meetings and corridor chats. At noon, Frank tidied the desk and brushed lint off his sleeve for the coming ritual. On Fridays he and the other solicitors met for a drink at Rabbitte's pub on Forster Street, a short walk from the office.

As Frank took the footpath downhill he remembered that he had yet to listen to that message from his wife. Everyone was on the second pint when he arrived at Rabbitte's, voices rising from a small circle at the corner table they reserved, jokes and anecdotes far from the hushed tones of legal conversation and the pared language of legal matters. Frank heard snatches of talk from the other tables too, people getting an early start to the evening:

We're going with the new house in Spain.

I hear Warsaw is still cheap. Buy an apartment now and rent it out.

Things have never been better.

One of his partners, Mr. Dukes, laughed with a raised glass to a joke and then nodded to Frank when he saw him bring a whiskey to the table. Frank took the seat opposite Dukes and sipped his first whiskey and nodded his way through the second, a dreamer in the threads of conversation. He was not listening to them. He wanted to tell them about what happened to him that morning, to ask if anything in their lives had ever disappeared when they weren't looking. It was a risk to say anything that personal to his colleagues when he probably did not know them as well as he thought, and to mention it might bring a slap on the back and a couple of extra drinks. Best say nothing.

Dukes called across the table, So what are your plans for the evening?

Frank told him about his wife's dinner party that evening and made a show of checking his watch and sighing.

Dukes said, Oh well, good luck.

I might have to miss it, Frank said.

Then you'd best have a drink while you're thinking about it.

Dukes waved to the bartender, and as the group fell back into talk, he pointed a finger to the table in emphasis as he leaned in a whisper to a junior solicitor.

The icon burned in Frank's pocket. He felt the weight of those weightless digital lines, the sound of the waiting voice trapped in them, whatever it was his wife said into the silent expanse that recorded her.

Whenever his colleagues asked about his wife, Frank said that she was fine, which was perfectly accurate. Nancy Delaney was still very pretty and a lot smarter than he was, the way she used exactly the right amount of words when she spoke, as if she had weighed them first. How lucky he was for the nineteen years with her, or any length of time, because those years replaced what would have been lonelier years and filled them with all the reasons people marry: for company, for love, for fear of not being married.

One night recently she brought home some property brochures that someone gave her at work. She was later than usual getting home and a little tipsy. She said that a second property was a good investment with interest rates so low, a good place for either of them to go to on weekends and holidays. She sat him down and pointed out some house styles and tapped the calculator with her pencil until the monthly payment showed in green numbers.

He said, Where are these properties exactly?

She said, In Westport. It's the next Galway, I hear. A site is available with a view and planning permission.

He said he would think about it and knew she would

bring it up again soon. Maybe that was the business wrapped in the icon.

The group at the next table grew louder by the minute in the afternoon cheer of a Friday:

Think of the early nineties even, it's so much better in Ireland now.

Things are grand all the same.

Frank checked his phone: still that envelope gleaming. He bought his round of drinks and made an excuse and then slipped out, searching his pockets for the keys. The taxis were busy already bringing people into town for the night out. Maybe he should stay in town. But it promised to be a warm evening and he decided to walk home. He could pick the car up tomorrow from the office.

The first ten minutes brought him through the city center. The light wind of summer blew along the line of sunlight and made a new man of him. This was his town and he should know it better. If he put his mind to it he could visit all his boyhood friends, make phone calls, write letters, go back to the school and get the addresses of his old classmates. By the end of the month he could easily contact most of the people he once knew.

He crossed the recently renovated town square, the benches and the grass lawn like a new oil painting whose original outline remained under the fresh paint: his own countless steps as a boy along these same streets. He stopped at the Skeffington Hotel and had another two whiskeys for the road, then crossed the street and walked with a certain swing in the arms down Shop Street and all the way to his former secondary school on Sea Road. He walked around the back to the playing field as the sun touched the spire of the church. Yes, still there: the stone seat near the handball alley where he'd smashed a ball around at break time, the same seat he watched from the classroom as he dreamed of the lunch break, of his chocolate bar. How hungry he was then, and how passionately he thought of that thin, cheap chocolate lying in his satchel under the desk. He tasted it a hundred times before he got a chance to eat it. He had not been that hungry in a long time.

Clouds moved across the sun as he retraced his steps back to Henry Street and took a right at Newcastle Road, heading for home, dodging first into another pub for a final couple of Jamesons until the rain from a single cloud thickened and fell away. A small crowd watched a rugby match and tightened into a cheer as a green jersey ran for the posts. Frank cheered along with them, raised his glass to the try. A happy fan slapped him on the back. This was a better crowd, but he had a home to go to. He gulped a quick couple of shots to let the rain blow itself out completely. The match ended and people drifted out. Frank left too, keeping to the wall to steady himself as more passing clouds spread shadows on the road. Thirty minutes later, and only ten minutes from his house, he passed the entrance to Dangan Park, where he checked his watch: close to five o'clock. He noticed the red banner strung across the park gates.

GALWAY CITY HOSPICE 8K RUN.

Frank thought he should watch the race and sober up, stay awhile and enjoy the cool breeze off the river that flowed a few hundred yards away across the fields. He hadn't eaten since the morning and the drink had gone straight to his head. He walked over to a throng of yellow and blue singlets, maybe fifty runners stretching in the shade. Some ran in place, some poked at wristwatches.

What are you doing here? I thought you had a dinner to attend.

The voice at his shoulder turned into Dukes, who leaned on the balls of his feet as if to balance the lemonade in his hand.

Frank said, I thought I'd walk home.

Dukes tipped the lemonade over to a thin girl in red and pink. My daughter's running today.

Then he turned to Frank, patted his belly and laughed through his large front teeth: Those running days are over for you and me.

Frank and Dukes had run in school together, and Frank once came second in the mile race at the school championships, pipped at the finish by the winner's cap. Some people who saw the race said afterwards that Frank should have been declared the winner. Now the drink loosened Frank's tongue.

What are you talking about, Dukes? Of course I could run eight kilometers. That's nothing. That's just five miles.

Dukes stopped in mid-laugh as Frank walked up to the registration table and held out a handful of cash.

He said, How much is it to run?

The boy dressed in the blue official jacket glanced all the way down Frank's suit to the leather shoes.

He said, The fee is ten euro, but the race is starting. You don't have time to change.

Frank said, I'll run a little bit to support the charity.

The boy came around the table and pinned a race number to the back of his suit.

From behind him Dukes said, Frank, I was only joking. Come on, Frank. You'll wreck the bloody suit for a start.

But Dukes was going to say that anyway. In school they had been rivals. Dukes had won that race because he wore a baseball cap. Maybe Frank could beat Dukes's daughter and settle the score. He stepped out into the late afternoon sun and joined the line of runners. He felt the bloat at his waist and undid his trouser belt, put it into his jacket pocket, retied the laces on his leather shoes and pulled the wool socks tight along his shins.

As he moved with the runners to the starting line, Frank heard Dukes call to him across the weeds in a combination of shout and whisper:

For goodness sake, Frank, you really need to think about this.

Frank hitched the ends of his trouser legs into his shoes and swung his arms and kicked his feet out in front of him to get some blood moving. He was sorry he'd worn the thick socks because now they'd bunch between his toes. And as for beating Dukes's daughter, she was far too young and fit for that. A warning sounded and everyone trotted to the white line on the grass and the front line leaned into the tape. The gun fired and the runners moved like a stretched elastic band from the serious ones up front to the walkers at the back. Frank kept up with the fast group as they wound through the gate away from the faltering claps of the spectators and into a much bigger field. He stumbled a few times in divots but pounded out some frantic steps to stay upright. Yet he was somehow in the second group as he rounded the first bend. The leading group was already well ahead. A pool of sweat formed low in his back and the wool socks bunched into wet sponges under his feet.

Once they approached the second mile, he had fallen from the second to the third group, the older runners. His armpits were soaked. Someone's shoe scraped his calf, and the tailor-made trousers clung soaked to his legs. His left shoe ran up and down the ankle and the skin started to flay, the pain like teeth. He hobbled, losing contact with the back of the third group and tried a burst of speed, opened his mouth wide to gasp his way to more air. The leather shoes were new and without mercy. He thrashed through the tall grass, smashing the dandelions, sneezing in the seed until he reached a gate, way behind the third group now but at least still ahead of the slowest runners.

A race steward waved and shouted something about no spectators being allowed in the race as Frank turned into a lane that ran parallel to the river for about five hundred yards before veering back into the connecting fields, where the slow runners ahead were already turning in a sleek line. He made it halfway down the lane and slowed under a stitch like a blade in his side. The puffs of the slowest joggers caught up with him as they all made the turn from the river and tramped across a field of red flowers.

They overtook him one by one, their shoes flicking the grass. He raised his knees as high as he could to get some extra speed, splintering the heads of the flowers as he pounded out a last great effort until his left shoe came off and he stumbled and then hit the ground knees first, filling the dandelions with his face.

Are you alright, someone shouted back.

The runners reached a low wall, jumped over it and disappeared. Frank lay alone with the sky above. Everything was so quiet so quickly. A cloud shade slipped down the slope. He grabbed stalks of weeds and wiped his face, then spat the seeds from his mouth and swung a hand through the flies that bobbed at his nose. After that he lay on his side and, hiding himself carefully between the flowers, urinated to such relief that he could have written about it. The sweat was a living thing, the tailored suit streaked with green.

At least one distinction was his: today he was the last runner. Then he heard talking and saw walkers come over the hill behind him, one of them pushing a pram. He sprang out of the grass, wiping the salt from his eyes and blowing his nose, and jogged back to the river where he scooped a few handfuls of water and drank. He tried to gauge how far he'd run: maybe four kilometers, three at the very least. He wondered if Dukes was going to hang around even after his daughter finished. Frank could not let himself be seen in this condition. He could run so slowly that all the spectators would have gone home by the time he arrived at the finish near dark in an empty field and to no one's approval, not a single hand clap, just a few people picking plastic cups off the grass.

No. As Frank ran through the gate that led from the river back to the fields he knew that he could not run to the finish line. But to leave the run early was unacceptable too—like putting a comma at the end of a paragraph. Under the hot evening sun he jogged right through some hedges and headed northeast, thinking he could run the rest of the race in a circle until he had covered the eight kilometers.

And so Frank Delaney, while not wanting to cheat like Dukes, ran the rest of the race on his own terms, dodging under trees, stepping in high and cut grass, through long and short fields until he had finished the distance. The sun had moved in the sky to where the shadows mixed with themselves, soon to be the one shadow of a single night. He moved into the open countryside beyond his house, the wide pastures that belonged to farms, where the sky seemed bigger above him even though the clouds had joined and poured brief showers in the distance like curtains over the water. He was tired of the sudden obsession with his past disappearing while he wasn't paying attention. The past was gone: that was the entire business of the past, and he should let it fall behind him gracefully now.

He left the park and walked until he stood at the door of his house shortly after six o'clock. Outside, four strange cars were parked on the street. He saw outlines in the lamplight through the curtains where, no doubt, his wife's dinner party was underway. Yes, that was a laugh just now, and that the clink of a glass. But he could not go in—the hallway passed the dining room, all open plan. He enters, they see him. The table falls completely silent: first his explanations, then their embarrassment, then his wife's fury at his appearance. There was nothing else for it, he had to wait.

Frank Delaney estimated that he had four hours to kill.

It occurred to him that he could finish the day the way he started it, by heading to a childhood home, but this time to the original family farmhouse he had lived in as a child, where he learned to take those first steps. The one his parents left to be closer to the city. If he kept up a good pace he would reach the farm in an hour. It was not madness but courtesy. He turned right and proceeded to fast-walk six kilometers north along the main road, where the farm was well hidden down a leafy lane.

After thirty minutes he sat on a low wall and took off his right shoe to straighten a loose sock, then shook a pebble from the shoe. The other shoe was ripped. Some raindrops stained the concrete. Cars passed and people rolled down windows to watch. He swung the jacket over his shoulder and continued, often straying from tiredness onto the road itself, but no one stopped to give him a lift, not even the ones who rolled down their windows and shouted at him to get off the road. He wrapped the sleeves of the suit jacket around his hips because he had a pain in the shoulder and he wanted to stretch it as he walked. Occasionally a car swerved to the middle and a horn blew and he stepped out of the way. By seven o'clock the cars streamed by, people with somewhere to go, all staring at him, but it was not strange surely to see a man out for a long walk.

Near eight o'clock he reached the lane. The sun was gone but still lit the sky. He found a gap in the hedgerow and moved through the adjacent field, where the ground was muddy and his shoes squelched under him. Cows swished their tails under low tree branches. Frank felt better. This was home country, the smell still familiar after all these years. Swallows swooped low in the humid air that soaked his shirt.

He placed one foot in front of the other and leaned forward, his arms swinging wider as he crossed the land to the main building. He remembered gathering hay one week when he was nine and the summers seemed longer than they were now. That was when he began to think of the farm as a living thing made up of the barns and the walls and the smells from the ground. That farm shaped thousands of his childhood dreams with its twilight shapes and frosty morning fields.

Frank arrived at the fence that ringed the family house and saw the place of his childhood for the first time in forty years, for he had never returned. In the driveway, a black Mercedes. An extension in progress to the main house. He went over every detail as if wrapping it carefully in paper: the sheds, the new roof, the professional design to the gardens. The living-room light glowed from behind drawn blinds, and he thought that he might still walk in and find his mother there. How many times had he seen that light as he ran to the house from the sanctuary of the trees and the long grasses? And how he had cried when they had to move to Galway so that his father could find a better job.

It was almost dark when Frank walked silently up to the kitchen window.

A child in a school uniform sat at a white table strewn with crayons over a sheet of paper under a lamp. Her tongue stuck out with the effort.

Frank put on his jacket again. The window was slightly open at the top and the child heard the noise: she looked up and cried in fright. Her mother ran from the living room.

What is it?

I saw someone out there, the child said, and pointed her crayon.

I'll see, the father said, and walked to the door. Frank watched motionless under the tree by the window as the front door opened and the father glanced into the night before returning to the kitchen.

Nothing there, you're seeing things that aren't there. He stroked his daughter's hair. It's all that drawing you do.

The child put her crayon on the table and took her page to the window. She pressed what she drew flat against the glass, a farmhouse with three people standing in it.

She said, This is a picture of our house. Go away.

It was shortly before ten o'clock when Frank was back at the main road south to Galway, his thumb out for a lift to the passing cars that droned out of the night. It rained suddenly and with force, a tropical shower. A young couple picked him up and dropped him a hundred yards from his house, and as he walked, each of the street lamps cast saucers of yellow light on the path in a series of rings that stretched down the footpath ahead of him. His wife's dinner party must be over now but for the conversation, or perhaps everyone had gone home.

As he stood in his doorway searching his pockets for the key he felt drenched again in warm air from the south. The street was quiet, with open windows and the avenues bordered in green trees and gently fluttering leaves. If green had a smell, this must be it, the heavy sweetness of a night rainstorm lifting off the trees and the grass. He listened for the laughter of guests, for muted music. Nothing. The house was dark.

He let himself in. The envelopes from the morning's mail were gathered neatly on the hallstand under the hall lamp, already sorted. His name was on all of those stacked. The rest his wife had taken away. He took out his phone and listened for the first time to the message the icon held. His wife's voice was kind and loving. It was a reminder that she was hosting the party. You are welcome to come, she said.

So simple. Why did he wait so long to listen to it?

But this was so many hours later, and everyone had been and gone. The dinner plates had been cleared from the dining-room table, and yet there was plenty of evidence that a gathering took place: the lingering smell of tobacco and wine, a plate of cheese left on the piano stool, the candles worn like eaten fruit, the chairs left awry when everyone stood to leave. A compact disc of Bach fugues lay on the chair next to where his wife always sat. He wondered why the chair next to hers was pointed to her chair. He wondered if the man who gave her the leaflets, the word on the properties in Westport, had come tonight. Perhaps that man was buying something in Westport too.

Frank gazed at the table and imagined the talking and the music, saw the faces blurred by the candle smoke and cigarettes. He took off the jacket and shirt and trousers, the shoes and socks, and sat on the chair at the table on the other side from the chair pointed to hers. He would not sit in a rival's chair. As he watched the last weak flames in the fireplace, he wondered what his wife would say if he told her that before going to work that morning he visited the house he once lived in, but saw the house that used to be there, not what it had become. He still saw the geraniums flowering in the garden, not a tarred parking space. What if he told her that while sitting in the privacy of his car on that street he had cried, suddenly and with great force, before he came to his senses and drove away to go to work. Was that what a successful solicitor does?

Now cold and wet, he wanted to ask somebody. He looked around the spent dinner table and an empty room and saw no one to ask.

One day some time ago, he went to a café and wrote in

a notebook the things he loved about his wife. If he compared that list with a list he wrote tonight, he might discover that some things were missing, but nothing he took away. He noticed recently that she was vague toward him. Without a doubt that was what happened when you lived with someone, you do not notice how they disappear inside the people they become. But he still loved the woman he first met, that happy, bright woman. He loved her with the loyalty that comes from not wanting to be alone.

Frank found himself looking down his folded arms at a wine glass above a white napkin wrapped in red string by a clean plate. To each side, a shiny knife and fork, everything undisturbed and symmetrical. One of her guests must have decided not to come.

The water from the shower stall turned hot and drained the glue of sweat and dirt from him. He hung the suit, the stained shirt and tie, the mud-coated socks, and stole into the dark and silent bedroom. With great care he eased himself onto the bed and lay on the covers for a while. Perhaps because of the relief that came with the promise of a night's rest, he soon whispered her name.

Nancy.

She did not stir. He touched her arm because he thought he heard her say his name, or was it the rain falling, and she moved her arm away from his fingers and under the blanket. He understood: the air blows through an open window and cools the skin.

What a day. Could he ever tell anyone about it? Not likely. He wanted to say that he loved her. He would say it first thing in the morning. He longed to reach for her across the bed. If he did, he was sure she would turn to him and smile in the night. Tomorrow he would also tell her how it was fine for them to buy the property in Westport—that he did not even need to see it first. It was not too late. But sleep was ending this day, reaching its numbing hands for him to fall into, and he resolved to remember these promises he made to her now in silence.

The bed was warm. Frank drifted and was lightly sleeping much later when he heard footsteps on the stairs. He watched the space under the door: it was his son, home a long time after him. Yes, there was the shadow walking softly past their bedroom. Yes, that was their son's door closing a square of light down to an inch of light, a handle turning softly shut.

BY IRISH NIGHTS

THEY FIRST APPEAR WHEN the sun is gone and the lights flicker in houses across the land, orange pins from windows that stick to the dark. The trees turn to shadows and the moon lights the country with a much weaker lamp as the first cars drive around, the drivers seeing few others on the roads in the late hour. They near the place and recognize the shape of the stone walls, the way the field and the sky distribute themselves generally. They continue because they cannot be late.

They talk as they have before, about tomorrow, about what happened yesterday. The night is quiet but for the tires that shear on concrete and on tar, the wind that blows in the open window, the music that stretches from the radio, all spread on different strands of sound, one above the other and clearer than ever. The white line moves at the side of the car or out into the middle until they move it back to the side with their fingertips. There is another car way off, they see the lights trail, but the road bends, and the beam is gone like a lighthouse they could end up following somewhere, but this place ahead is familiar, and besides, one of the other cars has come closer, out of nowhere, this huge light. And then it passes and they are driving again in the simple, long night.

Houses they know pass. A light in one has gone out, the light in the house of their parents, and they know that other mothers and fathers will soon be sleeping, they know how still a person can be in sleep and yet how so much can happen in that body, how many pictures and sounds and smells congregate in those women and men lying prone in beds or downstairs on couches, odd places where they hoped sleep might find them accidentally because they could not bring themselves to bed or do not sleep together anymore and therefore herd their dreams into separate rooms. Some have bottles by the bed, some keep bottles under the sink, some hide bottles inside themselves.

But there are so many places and so many cars. Across the country, from Donegal to Tipperary and down to Kerry, the roads have begun to fill, coast roads, roads through small towns, roads widening into the midlands, narrowing into cities, red signs, yellow signs, bump ahead, one hundred this, fifty that. So much to notice with a shoe on a pedal, a hand on a wheel, an eye on a road.

The night hour moves too on its own road, a wand passing through other numbers on the clock, and when the night drivers find the right place, the people in the cars move in circles, reverse and drive again, and they do this all night, or for as long as a night can feel. They are nineteen, they are twenty-four, they are six months old and on their mother's lap, there are pictures of them on mantlepieces. They are loved and they love. They call each other Mary, Fintan, Pamela. The drivers talk to pass the hours, speak of things that imprint themselves most on the mind from the seconds that make up a life: a glance, a birth, the smell of polished shoes, a forgiveness, an embrace stolen by hurry. To these images and sounds they return.

In the houses they pass some are not yet dreaming and do not see them go by, and many who are asleep have no interest in the countryside around, what was outside the car, and what inside those young people's lives brought them there at that precise moment. But there is no measuring the country in which these drivers move when the hour is late, because lost daughters and sons know that the certain few in those houses who lost them cannot dream of the dead, only of the living; and so the drivers dress in what they are remembered by, they speak the words they are remembered by. More cars on the roads as time passes, as the hand of the clock creeps to three, drivers in the distance, tens and then hundreds of cars a little way behind or approaching down a shadowy hill from the side. They remind themselves of the last journey they made, how they might have made another turn, waited another few seconds, done anything but drive to that place and at that time. They do everything you think when you dream of them.

From this same night other people come, some standing in unlit rooms, some walking the side of those same roads. Some hold a rope, some glance at pills in their hands. You can look all you want and wait for them to recognize you, say they know you. But they will not look back at you, will not look at you because everything is all right, this night is no different. I'm fine, they say. And then it happens, the words themselves come across the night to you: Why would things be any different tonight? They have spoken but not looked at you, and you know they've said these words to you who sleeps on this warm Irish night. You say they should have said something, and this one question slips from your sleep into the air and space and light that is special to dreams: Why couldn't you tell me?

But they have turned away, this son, this daughter, turned in spite, in loss, in love, in simple despair, and say that they never stopped telling you. But they must wait so that you can be ready with your help, with the help of certain doctors and friends gifted in the habit of listening, all summoned and arrived in time. Or you manage to save their lives by being somewhere different on that day, since it is a dream and therefore all things are possible to the grieving heart. This is not your time to hope. It is the way it happened. You lie in dread as they elude your best efforts, find a tree you'll find them in as soon as you wake and leave the house, a river that carries them away past the town buildings and into the sea, a sea with no memory. Other people, some older, walk these night roads, people who have no one to leave except themselves. They are unhappy, hounded, bored, will smile if someone passes, buy a newspaper as usual as breathing, make intricate plans for tomorrow that tomorrow will erase. Life has always been too much and too soon for them, or too little and too late. So many days in a row to wait for a better one.

No grief like this, the loss of children, no measuring it. Now that you are asleep their pain stabs for you through the mesh between death and life, it jumps a life and grabs for you when you can't move. It says, I hurt your child, now I am going to hurt you.

By Irish Nights

Past three o'clock—the middle of the night, and dark houses wrap the still bodies of the sleeping. Outside, the cars and the road walkers have dwindled to few. The moon strikes the western sea and foils it up against the cliffs. Some stars made of that same foil grab onto the black roof of heaven and hurt it into a shape. After the sun rises tomorrow and everyone wakes, the country will find a day bright and prosperous. Shopkeepers. The thump of newspapers. Ringing.

But not yet. In deepest night, before the dawn, some others stir out of the water, out of the sea at the shore, out of canals, rivers, lakes. They are not known to you, you never met them, and yours was a name they never heard. They come out of the dead of the night from the reach of decades, all because you read something in the café that day or the day before, yes, something from a newspaper held level to your eyes. The summer of 1961, eight boys and girls in West Cork.

In the middle of an evening they find the flat-bottomed boat at the water's edge and take poles and stand on it and shove the boat from shore. One of the boys gets his shoes wet and wants back. They swing back to shore and then set out again, now seven. They are not poor, they are not rich. They live in a country of the same jumper handed down for years and jam made from berries at the railway crossing, a country made of the walk to school, and their years pass in homework and the measure of bells. Three of them will stop, two at nine years, one at twelve. Their faces could be the faces of your own, faces scattered among black letters on a page, conjured into the living. They can live again when you dream them, feel the sun, how hot and thick it can lie on the wrist, how sharp the taste of fresh bread. But does it matter now who died, and so long ago, when you never knew them anyway.

This was the thing, they are wandering and it is a hot day and there is a boat at the water's edge, See, that one. Let's go in it and row it out to the middle. The poles don't touch the bottom and poke at water, no purchase. Help. The boat fills and swamps, they sink into the water and spread out and under, all struggling, kicking to rise. On shore some others see what is happening and swim to them and into mortal danger, clawing four to the steady grip of dry ground. But those three children. A small breath of water makes a sea of the lungs and sinks the breath.

They found themselves after in languid palms that rested upright in the still water, and they hadn't drowned. They found themselves in hands sometimes covered in swans that floated, shaped in rain drops that shook the surface of the sky where it rested on the water, in the hold of a father as he taught them to walk, in a mother's patience as she fed them from spoons and dressed them for the morning. And then they found themselves at last, carved into the endless hearts that lost them, waking every night to sleep.

ARCHEOLOGISTS

FROM WHERE THEY WORKED the road lay invisible, a five-minute walk away, where another shower wet the surface to a swish under the cars that slowed where it narrowed. Leading up to the eye of the needle the traffic was lined half a kilometer: a summer's night, people with an inch of patience and a place they weren't at yet. The headlights crawled in the lane along cones and construction signs before fanning into fours again as the road widened to the speed of open countryside.

The year before, a photo from a plane captured a swelling near the proposed petrol station and parking area off the new national road. A part of a pot was found in the ground not far from where the bog began. A private consulting company in Dublin won the license to excavate and hired the couple on the site as temporary summer archeologists.

Robert glanced above the dig wall and angled his wristwatch into the fading light.

It's almost ten, he said, and stared across the field at the restaurant on the other side of the road. The lights were on in the windows and he saw the shapes sitting at tables sipping from glasses by candlelight, eating food on plates with the motion of steel forks and knives and elbows. There must be music too, they always had music on Friday nights, he could almost hear it, fiddle music, and he and Emma would be there in a very short while, they would run across the field with bicycle lights in their hands and arrive just in time, as they had every Friday night for most of the summer, but for now all he had was those distant and silent shadows behind the glass of the restaurant windows.

The raindrops tapped the tarpaulin spread above them on timber supports. Because it was the end of the summer Robert felt colder, felt the night coming and thought what it would be like as a real night, without lights and without a warm place to spend it. He hunched his shoulders and turned to the woman on her knees in the bottom of the pit.

They'll be closing the kitchen in half an hour, he said.

From where she crouched, squinting at the flecks of stone she sifted in the damp clay with her brush, Emma felt the thread of annoyance in the voice behind her—she had not responded to what he said about the time because it was not a question. She stood and lit the bulb that hung from the rope and the electrical wire twisting around it from the generator. Framed by the conical shade, yellow light filled a wide circle at the bottom of the pit. She turned and held a hand over her eyes and spoke to where he stood by the trench wall.

I need to do another two inches, I'll be fifteen minutes. If you want to you can go ahead.

Robert moved into the light. But we'll miss the kitchen even if you're only fifteen minutes. It's another five to clean up and five to walk. What time does that leave?

Emma bent again with the brush, heard the sigh and closed her eyes.

You can order for me, I'll be there. They stay open longer anyway.

Are you still there? Emma said.

Robert was watching a white shirt approach with a flashlight held between the squelch of steps and a soft curse. It was Touhy, the construction foreman, arriving from the main roadworks. Usually he wore impatience in the guise of curiosity. All over the country, two thousand archeological digs were ongoing, most of them private firms working ahead of construction to get the objects out of the ground, file a report and cover the site up so that the concrete could be poured. This evening there was no disguise: he stood at the ramparts and eyed Robert.

Well, where are we?

Mr. Touhy, Robert said.

Touhy glanced past him at Emma. Where are we? We want to finish this by next weekend. We have to start the parking area by next weekend, so this will have to be finished and filled in by then.

Robert said, I'd say we're another two days at the most. We'll have the artifacts recovered and the site report done on Wednesday morning.

That's five days, Touhy said, still looking at Emma.

Two business days, Robert said. But we're aware of the interests involved.

Touhy traced the ground back to Robert and lifted his eyes and his voice.

Every day is a business day for me. He pointed behind him at the bulldozers parked black against the low light in the sky: Those machines are costing me an arm and a leg, the crew, the delay, three months now. So what's the story?

Touhy lately came at the end of every day, as if they needed to report to him before going home. Emma had taken to calling him a bully. She spoke from the dirt.

An archeological dig is not a delay. We need three days.

Touhy said, Three days now? It was two a minute ago.

The rain fell harder on the white shirt. Emma stood in the bulb light and counted out fingers. Three, and it will be four if you keep us from working long enough.

The developer pointed behind him again. I have two machines and a whole crew waiting to build. Look out there, he said.

She followed his hand to the shapes of the bulldozers, parked off the new road, black and huge against the sky, steel insects frozen to the shape they stopped in.

Touhy's voice rose: This is thousands a day for me.

Robert stood between them. We're practically done here, he said.

Emma wasn't sure if he had spoken to Touhy or to her.

No, we're not almost done, she said.

Touhy took out a mobile phone. Dublin wants to know what's going on. We were made promises, assurances by your employers. I'm calling Dublin.

He walked back into the night, his face a ghost in the glow of the phone, looking for people in a city already gone home for the day. Touhy disappeared back into the night until only his shouts reached them.

The way you can't be rid of some people, Emma thought. Some people leave a trail of themselves wherever they go.

Robert turned to her. You can't do that again, Emma. We have to work with these people.

What you mean is we're working for them now.

In a way, yes. That's the way it is. We have to keep ahead of them.

The first stars were blotted by a cloud. A breeze moved the bulb.

Can't you steady that thing? he said.

It'll settle after the shower, she said.

It's a long shower.

She shook her head and knelt again.

Go ahead, Robert. Order for me, will you? I'm sorry, I'll be along. They'll wait in the kitchen, they know us.

She waited for him to walk along the raised plank and leave her in peace, but he did not move, did not speak, shuffled behind her. The brush in her fingers was the loudest thing in the world, rasping over the grains and the specks of stone and eventually across their silence.

He cleared his throat. What about next weekend? My parents want to know, I don't really mind myself, it's them.

What about next weekend? she said.

He said, For god's sake, Emma. The dinner at my house to celebrate the end of the dig. My uncle and aunt will be coming. I told you about it last week. You said you'd tell me today.

This was exactly what would wear her down in the end, the questions about her plans, so many and so many the same. She and Robert met at the university. He was an only child from a rich family, she was one of six and paid for everything after secondary school. He lived with his parents, she shared an apartment near the diving tower in Salthill.

She sifted away under the bulb. It was his voice but his parents' questions: they wanted to make straight lines out of their son's future, and they wanted to put their son neatly into that future, or her into his, and they did not give up easily. They viewed her completely through his interest in her— she was more their son's future wife rather than a real woman to them. The reverse though was equally true, because to her they were Robert's parents rather than a woman and a man, and she didn't like them or their disappointment that their son had chosen, as his mother put it one evening at a dinner, 'a beautiful, independent woman', as if Emma might bring him sorrow because of her consistency, her looks, her focus. For the sake of a happy marriage those qualities should be his.

He had still not left for the restaurant.

She said to the ground, What did you say about next weekend?

If you're coming.

I don't know. Maybe.

Just for the evening, you'll be back by eleven.

Okay then, she said.

Excellent, I'll let them know, he said. He walked to the jacket hanging on the hook on the post. And the weekend after that, the holiday weekend?

She closed her eyes. Without a response, perhaps he might stop.

He slotted one arm and then another through the oilskin sleeves, and shook till it rested comfortably on him.

My parents want to know because we're planning a trip to Donegal, the house there. We'd have plenty of time to ourselves, of course.

Why do they have to know if I'm going?

Because they've invited my uncle and aunt, so you would make four of us and my parents.

But why do they have to know now?

Plans, they like to plan, I know that annoys you. It's good manners to give them an answer, Emma. Yes or no?

That's pure pressure, Robert.

It shouldn't be, you don't have to feel that way.

But I do.

Have you other plans, is that it?

No.

He stuck his hands into the pockets. Then?

I want to keep that weekend open.

She had nothing to put into that future weekend, but she didn't want it filled with a trip to Donegal, the silence in the car after his parents ran out of questions that met with one-sentence answers, the rage at being cooped up when she could have been reading a book, looking out the window at the sea, or going out on the town for the night with her friends. She felt that she was losing them, the handful of girls she would so desperately miss if they passed that invisible line of lost friends, a line you get to see only after you've crossed it. That wasn't going to happen, not for anyone.

But my parents like you. It'll disappoint them.

She rose, turned, grabbed his arm and held it. I want to keep my plans open.

My parents will feel slighted.

She met his eyes. I'm sorry, Robert.

Don't apologize to me, I don't feel that way, but they've been nice to you, haven't they?

Yes, and I'm sorry they'll feel put out.

He folded his arms, tightening her hand inside them. I suppose it's too early to talk about Christmas.

She pulled her hand back. He was becoming another man to her, young men who lose what they want through their urgency to get it.

I'm going, he said.

Robert walked across the field to the roadworks but without the bicycle light which he left behind in his annoyance. Why couldn't she come with him? Above the scratch of trees some weak light blotched the night, the tip of a white paintbrush edging the sky, not enough to see by, but he knew the way: on Friday evenings for the past ten weeks he and Emma had tramped this way together, across the field and the last phase of the new road between the dual carriageways east of Galway. It was not a disputed development. There was no glen nearby, no view to be spoiled, no pressure groups arguing for a different route, just a well-planned road running through a flat piece of land, and if any place ever were made for a road, it was this place. The construction company had been happy with the progress. The topsoil clearance revealed nothing of architectural value, and when they cleared the sod and ploughsoil, they found nothing. But then came that photograph taken from the air, the swell in the ground where the petrol station would be. The test trench produced Neolithic stone and everything stopped. The exact spot was a four meter pit where the field gave way gradually to a bog.

Touhy, the owner of the construction firm, had been beside himself when they arrived at the beginning of the summer: a small stretch holding up the parking area for the station and therefore the entire development—the injustice of it—not even the road itself but a ramp off it.

Robert came to the empty bulldozers parked by the road, buckets arched to the sky, and he watched the single file of cars sweeping past and waited for a driver to see him and stop to let him cross, but the oilskin made him hard to see. The wind increased between temperatures, blowing the coat about his head. After two minutes he ran across. Rubber skidded and a horn blew long and loud after him as he made for the lights.

At the restaurant Robert tried the door and found it locked. He knocked, and when no one answered, he knocked louder three times. The door opened an inch and the voice said, Sorry, we're closed.

Robert held his watch up to the crack, But it's not ten.

Sorry, the kitchen is closed, open again at nine tomorrow morning.

The door creaked shut. Robert knocked again. After a pause the voice said *closed* slowly.

He leaned his forehead to the frame. We just work across the way, he said. Come on, we've come here every Friday evening for ten weeks.

Then you know we close at ten, the muffled voice said. After he knocked once more a face replaced the voice, the head waitress, he remembered her from other nights.

She glanced at him and the empty parking spaces for someone else.

Who's we? she said.

He turned and looked into the dark, looked for the pit across the traffic cones.

Emma, she's coming. By the time the order is ready she'll be here.

If she were here at this moment you could come in. I heard you say *we*, and I see only you.

The door shut for the second time. Another sheet of rain fell, a chord of drops spreading fingertips across the strings of the dark to strum one wet hiss on the path around him. Robert moved to the side of the building and stood at a window: at least five couples sitting, more he was sure if he strained his head, and a waitress carrying a meal on a trolley to a table, a candlelit, lace-covered one in the corner that he and Emma always chose. At a different table a man poured from a bottle of red wine. The music was as clear as if he were inside. He and Emma had so much to talk about tonight, and this was the place, not back there in the pit but where conversations and plans belonged: music, drink, food, shelter, light, all the elements of life in one place. He could smell the subtle perfume, he was sure of it, and hear the rustle of talk, the folded dress of conversations over the tables. He placed his hands on the glass as a waitress passed with a plate of chocolate cake. When he tapped on the glass she looked at him and shook her head. Robert waited till she returned from the table and tapped again. She walked to the window, showed him her watch—four minutes past ten—and arched her eyebrows. When he motioned to the door and shrugged, she drew the curtains.

You bastards, he shouted. After all the business we gave you.

He huddled to the concrete as the wind blew the main part of the shower over the restaurant with heavier drops.

Archeologists

What an end to the last weekend of the summer, shouting at curtains. Someone laughed inside and a new song played.

He was worried about Emma. He was worried about his parents. Not because they had rejected her, nothing that obvious, more the understanding they gave him that they wanted him with someone else, and lately they never mentioned her except when Robert did. He insisted they be nice to her, that they invite her to trips and dinners. His mother explained that they tried to befriend her but met with a serial cold indifference and had given up. They did not want her to dinner next weekend or on the trip to Donegal because she strained the atmosphere. They were waiting for him to move on, to lose his interest in 'that particular girlfriend', as his father put it. Robert felt himself standing in the middle of everyone's expectations, waiting for Emma and his parents to accept each other, arranging for as much contact between them to close the mental distance. Surely that strategy would work in time. He hated how irritating his entreaties seemed to his parents, how weak and petty he must seem to Emma.

He tried to make out where the pit was, saw nothing. Was that a gleam? Perhaps, but the passing beams from the cars outshone any small lamp that glowed in the far field. The traffic thinned then and in the space of those few seconds . . . yes, way out there, that was the tiny prick of the bulb. He loved her isolation, how unattainable she was in so many ways, as lost to him when they worked side by side as she was now, under that spark and the endless western night. He walked back into the night, leaving the warm and safe couples inside that concrete and under that roof behind him. He ran across the road and slowed as the mud found his boots and began to grip. This was the season of shorter days, dusk falling sooner across the weeks. A few feet in any direction and he was without direction in this utter dark. The more the builders filled the countryside with roads, the more lost he felt. And he was part of it. But it was for the best, and in any case the dead don't need explanations.

As he came to the pit again, the floating faint glow of a mobile phone projected the ghost of a white shirt and a voice: Yes, I'm still here, I'm still waiting.

Touhy saw Robert and waved the phone, I'm waiting for Dublin. This madness has to stop. The whole summer and we're still here.

The foreman walked around behind the tarpaulin to the other side of the shelter.

On her knees in the clay, Emma saw the gleam of the phone pass to her side. Touhy again, the raging idiot, every sentence out of him a step closer to something he wanted. Otherwise he said nothing. There was a ruthless logic to it. The trick was not to let him get to her. She was thinking about him only because she could see him, and just as quickly she could forget him. Touhy walked away into the night, his breath a flowing stain over his head.

Robert walked down into the pit. Emma saw his frustration immediately. He was attractive, there was no other way to describe him, that smoldering look, and his annoyance only accentuated it. Perhaps that was all that held her to him, maybe she was that shallow. Left alone in the cold and dark pit while he went to the restaurant, she had thoughts and then second thoughts about leaving him: His parents were rich and there was talk of support if they married, a comfortable house, the down payment arranged, and in the vast expense of modern Ireland, that was a very good start. Yes, she wanted to own her own house first before marrying anyone, marry first her own space and silence and only then someone else's. But she did not have the money and she never would, house prices had risen too fast. She cursed her fear of being alone when that was all she wanted. His parents obviously wanted her to marry him. Maybe she should.

The restaurant is closed, Robert said. They wouldn't wait. Where were you?

Look, she said, and pointed to the ground.

What? Robert moved closer under the bulb and his shadow curled about her.

She said, Only these last few inches. Don't you want us to finish? She looked down at the brush, the grains of soil and tiny flecks of stone.

Robert shook his head, lifted his wrist to the illuminated hands of a watch.

We're coming back next week.

No, she said, I want to finish it tonight. I can't be around that man. He'll wear me out, he knows what he's doing.

But the report, Robert said. I have to write the report and you're not even close to finishing tonight.

The assessment report will take you thirty minutes. I've seen the ones you've written, a few paragraphs no one will read anyway and that's the end of it, the builders move in.

You want to finish the excavation tonight?

Yes, she said. What's the point anyway? Nothing will change what's about to happen here.

But it's our last job for the summer. Shouldn't we try to make it last?

She moved the brush again in darts at the end of her loose fingers. You're in my light, Robert.

He stood aside, folded his arms and unfolded them as the wind turned the tarpaulin into a lazy sail that swelled and buckled.

At least, he said, have you thought about what we're going to do?

But Emma was thinking of something else, an incidental conversation they had about their family trees at the beginning of the summer. Robert could trace his ancestry all the way to the Normans, but she was Nordic, some of her, and the rest was uncertain. A dream she had in midsummer still dangled its loose threads into her waking hours when the rest of the world pressed in on her. In the dream she was four feet down into a bog, slicing away in a trench until she came to a slab of stone; she lifted it to one side with the strength of a dream. From below a perfectly preserved woman stared up at her, five foot six, blond hair in braids at the high forehead, blue eyes open, a gold necklace draped on her strong white shoulders, a woman who matched her appearance in the way that she might be gazing at the surface of a clear pond, and as she stared in fear and in joy, she thought that surely such a thing must happen in time, that a copy of everyone is born across the centuries. Yes, this was the dream she had, that when she dug through the bog she found herself, surrounded by flints she used when alive, wearing a necklace she may have made, and she saw that she was untouched by decay. So she bent to touch both hands, they were cold, she rubbed them, the fingers held hers gently; she slid off her clothes and then lay down on top of herself, and the woman moved and they embraced, said the same name to each other. She could remember even now what it felt like to make love to herself, to kiss her own breasts, to cup her face in her hands and slide her tongue into her own mouth, to smell the scent she used, to feel safe without a secret between them, to settle into the curve of her own belly, to feel those hands in her hair, this woman who lived and died and lay still for hundreds of years under Vikings, under monasteries, under every occupation. None of it meant a thing to Emma beyond the beauty of that high forehead, the way the blue sea was arranged in her eyes, an ancient kindness. And there would never be a word between them except that one name, no other words that kill everything they touch. Because she had found herself, she did not need words.

Well, have you thought about it? Robert said. I feel as if I'm talking to myself sometimes around you, Emma.

Instead of answering she mentally checked off the boxed catalogue of items they had uncovered under the swelling that the waiting mechanical diggers could flatten in four minutes: three earthenware pots, a deer antler, a flint scraper, a bone pin two and a half thousand years old, give or take a few hundred years.

I'm thinking about it still, Robert.

He was briefly and unconsciously a father. She had told him nothing: It was none of his business, she did not want to join their lives together using a third life. She took a pill and the child went away, left much regret and so silently in the space it made, and her body went back to being single without visible signs—no trail of instruments, no hands, no eyes searching her, no waiting rooms. The journey to being hollow was water in a glass. When something tiny fell from her into the toilet, she did not look. She flushed the cold handle and washed her face.

He was ambitious and finished his doctoral work ahead of her ways to warehouse the massive data unearthed because of the construction boom. He composed it mostly on the computer in his bedroom. She had read and reread drafts, heard the central idea emerge from the rough writing into polished prose above countless cups of tea. He gave his first public speech at an archeological conference in Kilkenny to debate the crisis in Irish archeology. She had not heard the final draft of his dissertation until then, and the language bothered her, nothing like the passion of the first efforts he read to her from the folds of the blankets on his bed, but a style that rose above everything it described, English designed to say just the right amount of nothing.

We thought there were five hundred thousand at most, he said at the lectern with that earnest face above the tie and the shirt. But because of accelerating construction to meet the demands of the new economy, we now suspect there may have been a million people alive at one time in Stone Age Ireland.

At the end the audience spattered into claps. Some figures rose and walked to him, important people, judging by how pleased Robert was afterwards. In recent years she had fallen away from the politics of archeology to the work itself. These were the final years of opportunity for someone like her, a field archeologist. What was left of those people was in clay, under fields, a marker here and there, stone codes even professionals didn't fully understand, a language of leaving things. When the country had finally exhausted its store of the past, maybe someone like Robert would oversee the interpretation of what had been dug up. She preferred the dirt on her fingers, the smell of the bog. *The lady of the bog*, he called her once, and it pleased her.

She left him to his admirers and passed along the hall to the pub next door. Robert came in with two men and they entered the next booth, where a discussion blew up around cups of tea. Through the opaque glass two voices leaned in argument. The man with a beard like smoke said to Robert, But you work for a private company. You excavate in no time and write a short report, stick the stuff in a warehouse. Why not share what we're finding with the public? We're digging them up and hiding them again.

The man to Robert's left shook his head: All in time, I'm sure. We can't stop the building, everyone knows that.

The rain was down again upon them, the tarpaulin lifted and fell.

Robert coughed. So what will we do? If we finish the work tonight, when will we see each other again? I have to start in Dublin next week.

You'll be down on the weekends, she said. We can call each other.

Call each other? What does that mean?

Emma sighed. It means what I said. I'll dial a number and you'll answer, or the other way around.

She stood and went to him. He missed her already, she could tell, perhaps it was because they hadn't had sex in a week. That was easily fixed. Maybe that was why he had this notion about the restaurant, to get her in the mood before he went back to his parents and she to her small apartment. She turned away from him and pulled his arms around her waist and pressed herself into him. He slid his hands higher, under the overalls and across her belly. She felt the soft circle of his lips on her neck, he breathed her name into her hair. She saw the glint below her and looked down: his wristwatch. The second hand slammed into the next slot and tumbled forward into another. His touch was too heavy, an archeologist shouldn't have a heavy touch. She was going to leave him. The when and how were invisible to her as yet, the reason had not formed in her mind, but she knew that soon they would part and the reason would not matter. She was going to leave his fear of empty weekends, leave the metronome of his parents' questions measuring everything she and Robert did.

She reached for the brush and stepped forward an age from his fingertips. They slid from her.

Nothing his family said or did would ever change her mind. She was late thirty-five, he early twenty-seven, twenty-five hundred odd days between them, that was all, but she would be thirty-eight when he was still in his twenties. As she got older she wanted to know more about her grandparents and their parents. The more she discovered about them the better she would know the present, her own illnesses, her own temperament—as if portions of her life had been already lived for her, the same weak ankle, the same feeling of restlessness of early autumn evenings, the sunlight at a certain time of day across the town—those mysteries that were appearing in her life that could be solved only by returning to the people who lived before her. She felt that there were things she could only know when she reached the age of her parents. But they were both dead of bad hearts, and she had never really sat down and talked with them about their own parents, and so that bridge was gone too. With a pile of photographs she tried to piece a history of the wider family together. The images lay in pieces in her hands, figures of people beyond speech, and without a living being to point and talk to her, she felt distant from the people she belonged to. She had studied half her life away and forgot to look up. She was as alone as that buried woman in her dream.

When they drove back to Galway after the conference he was happy, she could tell, happy with the new contacts, another step to a position in government. And shortly after the conference he was offered the job in Dublin. She found herself looking out the side window as he talked about what he would achieve in the first year, a new publishing house for archeological reports, fifty a year.

She tried to imagine all those people. They had covered the country three thousand years ago. There had to be towns, villages, the old Irish dug up from the ground, and now the new Irish were hiding them again, burying them in long, dark warehouses and reports. Perhaps it was because he didn't have the subtle pressure of rent that Robert's officiousness itself seemed rented, and she wasn't sure where the real man was in him. She had been waiting for that man to emerge.

On that Sunday drive they stopped at an outdoor café. The sun was warm and Emma pulled off her blouse to a white T-shirt. Robert ordered the champagne from the bottom line of the menu.

She leaned across, saw the number opposite the drink. Jesus, Robert. Can we afford that?

I can, he said and folded the menu closed.

She laughed behind her sunglasses. The champagne mixed with the sun and buoyed up the world for both of them. They knew again why they were together for the rest of that day. They got up at two the following afternoon and spent hours walking the beach. Robert seemed quieter, something on his mind. As for her, to get that conference out of her system she wanted to find a simple language again, find one that she and Robert could share. Perhaps that was why on the beach she came up with a scheme which she turned to explain to him.

She said, There should be a glass case where we show what we found and where, no explanations or terminology, the way you don't put explanations on a photograph of your family.

A glass case? Robert said, squinting at the Burren mountains from the shore. It was one of those Galway afternoons, blowing the sun around in the sky, flinging seabirds in fists low across the promenade.

She said, Maybe just the date they lived. You stand looking at it and then look around at the hill or the river they may have seen when they lived.

I don't understand, Robert said.

I'm saying we should not send artifacts away to Dublin or anywhere. We should recover the evidence and leave it where we find it, at every roadside stop, in each new housing development. Build glass cases and put the material in them, their knives, their pots, what they placed in their hair to keep it neat. Show how thousands of years ago, so many people lived here. People *lived* here, Robert. And when you stand at those cases you can look around and see the same horizon. It would be so comforting.

Robert said nothing for a few seconds, concentrating on the line of the mountains across the bay as if studying what she said for hidden meanings or traps. He found none.

That's romantic, Robert said. That's almost what I'd expect from a child. I'm surprised at what you say sometimes.

Their talk was replaced with silence, the way the silence becomes a living thing that stands asking, Well, what now?

She broke that silence. What we're doing to our own past, there's a price.

Robert looked at his shoes. I understand, I really do. But I was going to ask you to marry me today.

Oh, Robert, I'm sorry—

And that's why I'm worried.

About what?

That if I ask, you'll say No.

She leaned her forehead into his shoulder as the sun swept along the sand toward them, across seaweed and from the blue sky through the screeching wings.

Don't ask me just yet.

She felt him nod, and they spent the rest of that Monday strolling through the streets and alleys of Galway, as if remembering it as a couple, committing the buildings and walls to their mind in case this was their last time.

Now, in a rainy pit at the onset of night, he stood silently behind her. The dig was ending. He was starting a new job in Dublin. He had asked her about her plans a number of times, and now he wanted to know. There was no getting out of this, no buying time with vague phrases about waiting. She had to tell him one way or the other, and the time was now.

The little flakes of stone and soil could have been distant planets at the end of her brush, so far away they seemed, so uncollected her thoughts. What Robert had said that day at the beach. He was right. Though a trained archeologist a season away from her doctorate, her inclinations at times were romantic, and Robert, if she voiced them again, would not approve. He would never approve, and marriage would not change that. Those distant tiny planets tumbled around at the end of her brush: She wanted to bridge the gap somehow. But those people from the past did not speak loudly enough about themselves. She needed to find something that was written in a previously undiscovered Neolithic script, a recording etched into stone instead of a round metal disc, something that said, This is what we did, this is where we were, and here are pictures, here are the sounds of our voices, this is who we fought, this is who we loved and who loved us. Now you know.

And this was what drove her. Had they felt then what she felt now? Was feeling itself handed down in the genes, like clothes? What if she and Robert uncovered the find of the decade, a stone showing a connected series of villages and roads.

She remembered a row about what to call Ireland at the conference. It started in back rooms during sessions when someone said that because of immigration it was important to protect Irish national identity and its cultural heritage before they were lost. Someone objected: any reference to a national identity was exclusionary and racist. Over many cups of tea the term was changed to island identity, and then regional identity, which was carried over to the general session. After a divided vote, it was Robert who proposed a compromise wording, the need to protect Irish regional characteristics.

She said, We talk a different language, Robert. We use different words for the same things. It troubles me so much, I'm worried that we'll be different in everything.

She turned and smiled and put her hands around his face and kissed him.

Robert hugged her. Why are you putting yourself through this?

Because I want to know now, not in twenty years in some warehouse, I want to know what they had in their hands every morning.

He said, We will, I promise you. We'll go through what's been found and we'll find some way to publish the findings, the context, everything. Will you leave with me? I don't want you alone with Touhy, though I think he's given up.

Touchy, she said. Mr. Touchy? He's not going anywhere. He'll be back.

His name is Touhy. That's so childish.

But now Robert was laughing too.

Come here, he said. Look up there.

She joined him at the trench wall. The sky briefly cleared and the stones of the night shone, constellations, the blur of the Milky Way.

Isn't it wonderful? Emma said. With one glance you see faster than time.

Then she looked behind them, back to the pit. She said, Why do we always see the past as down?

What? That's where it's preserved, he said. You're in a strange mood tonight. I'm hungry. He cast his eyes to the restaurant, the lights, the cars parked there people outside, wine, pizza, all across the dark field, the faint smell of bog.

Wait a minute, he said.

She watched with him. Yes, some people were leaving the restaurant, their laughs thin on the night air. But others were being ushered in with a quick arm.

Robert said, I swear they're letting people in. What the hell is that? Let's run over and break in the door. Let's just smash in the door and run into the kitchen and take what we want.

She smiled. That was a man she could marry. Do you mean that?

He said, Of course not. We'd be arrested on the spot. But this is outrageous. I should make a complaint, write a letter to the owner.

She said, We'd not be arrested on the spot. Out here in the sticks? The police would take, I don't know, at least twenty minutes to get there, more like half an hour.

And?

And you could hold the owners off with a frying pan while I went through the cupboards and cooked a meal for us both. We'd take it to the table we always sit at and eat it. We can pay them at the end, if that's what worries you.

He shook his head.

She said, I thought so.

Robert looked puzzled. You didn't want to go there a

few minutes ago, and now that's all you want. When are we going to get married?

It was the first time he asked. She stepped back. I'm not ready to get married to anyone.

I meant to me. Us getting married.

We don't need to be married, she said.

It was not her speaking. The oldest rituals said it to her from the depths of the ground. There was nothing marriage brought that you didn't already have, you still shared what you had. Why was he still interested? Perhaps she was a test he could not pass and for that reason studied harder.

His voice softened at her shoulder: We are alive now, this is our time. I love you, Emma.

I know.

Then why can't you come to the dinner?

She was fastened to something. If rock can gleam, pale rock, was that rock gleaming from the clay?

Robert. Give me thirty minutes and I'll leave with you. We can go back to my place. You can stay with me, we can drink a little wine and watch a long film.

That would pacify him.

I think we should not see each other for a while.

The words were Robert's, not hers, and they floated across the pit to where she was on her knees sifting again.

She nodded. Okay, Robert.

She heard his silence.

He said, Is that it, *Okay*?

Emma turned to him: Can we talk about this later? Can you help me now?

No, I'm not doing this any more. It's dark, it's wet, we're not supposed to work like this, it's not good science.

Emma took his arm and brought him to the trench wall and pointed into the dark where two shapes carved out a darker piece of the sky for themselves.

See those two machines waiting over there? They don't do science, she said. And next week they're coming this way, and where you and I are standing will be a parking area for a petrol station. Don't talk to me about good science.

He took her hand off his arm. Don't patronize me. Don't fucking patronize me. My parents don't even want me to invite you anywhere. I'm doing this impossible dance between all of you and I'm tired of it. Do what you want.

He walked to the shelf where they kept their things and shook out his good shoes.

I'm going home.

She put her face in her hands and shouted through her fingers. Go home to your mammy and daddy. Go on home.

That's not fair, he said.

Go home and watch television with mammy and daddy.

Look, I'm sorry you lost your parents, Emma. Jesus I'm sorry.

I didn't lose them. They died. They're dead. They're rotting in two holes. That's where my parents are. Don't use words like *lost*. I can't stand it. Say what it is.

He sighed. I don't think I like you sometimes.

She nodded into her hands.

It was bound to happen. One of them was going to say something, and it didn't matter who, not really. You say goodbye or he does, all the same in the end, a matter of brief pride. That's what she said twice into her hands.

So what do you want to do, Robert?

He said, I can't write the report until the excavation is complete. I'll come on Monday and review the site and write it. If you're here, I'll see you then.

Emma moved back to her brush, her arm mechanical in its motion. To an untrained eye, she was returning to her usual work in the usual manner, and that was her answer to what he said. But through her hands she had definitely seen something in the ground whipped bare by the wind, a film of soil cleared away. A rock, the top edge of a rock. Of course the ground was full of rocks, but this one appeared to be two rocks at right angles. She whisked hard to clear on each side, but the brush was not enough. It would take a few days like this, so she dug around it with her fingers.

What are you doing? Robert said.

Emma gouged a handful and threw it to the side.

I said what are you doing?

I see something, she said. Where's the pickax?

Over there. You can't use a pickax, you'll destroy everything.

Emma took one step, grabbed it from the wall, took the same step back and swung it high and down, not in the direction of the ground but into the trench wall itself.

Are you insane? Robert shouted.

The diggers will do the same, she said, so what does it matter? We don't have time. She swung again and sliced out stones and packed clay. Let's not pretend to be anything but what we are, diggers ahead of the diggers.

No, Robert said, waving what seemed to be three arms. This is wrong, we can apply for an extension. He grabbed the handle but she pushed him back and his eyes groped to take in all the surprise as he fell back and hit the other wall. In what would have taken the best part of a week, she gouged chunks of it and took a stick and poked around the rock on the ground.

Will you help me, she said. We need something to show first.

He said, I can't be involved in this.

She went head first into the space, grabbing stones and heaving them behind her into a pile, working with the stick in smaller spaces, much of it by feel because there was no light where she worked. She was with them now, she was in the place where light had been and long left. This was why she studied years to be an archeologist.

She heard Robert behind her: I won't report this if you stop now.

The voice of a stranger. Robert would balance her and his career, and she would lose. To hell with her doctorate. After five minutes she stopped and went back to him.

The burial chamber was a meter wide and long, made by a ring of rocks. A thin wide slab covered it.

She said, Will you at least help me lift it?

They moved together, it came off easily and they moved back. He caught the dangling electrical wire and lifted the bulb nearer the hole.

They stood in what would shortly be the edge of the parking area at the side of the petrol station on a ramp off the main road. The chamber lay a few feet from the place where the chemicals of bog might have preserved some of the body, given them a good idea of what the person looked like, perhaps the color of hair. Instead of leathered skin, they had a skeleton. But bones too tell a story to a field archeologist, where the wear is, what kind of burdens in life damaged certain joints, or someone who did not have to work, what kind of food wore down the teeth on which side of the mouth. All those years buried in books were not for nothing.

But then her seeing changed. The stillness stirred inside her and laid its hands upon her, and she could not move.

This isn't happening, Robert said. This never happens. What were they doing here?

The place was clean and protected, and the bones had survived. Emma's eyes welled up with emotions in the moisture that blurred her sight.

She was crying for herself. She was getting old. She would live on her own. There would never be a time when she was not on her own. What if she had kept the baby? Maybe she should have kept the baby. She cried for a child she had never met, she cried for her parents, she cried for herself.

With one glance across time she saw the skull, the shoulders, the spine curled in two short strands that wove through shallow muck. A mother had cried for a long time after this child died. Three thousand years ago was yesterday: she was buried here, exactly as she lay.

Despite the tears, Emma had registered at once the shape and was already convinced.

It's a girl, she said.

The storm flapped and the tarpaulin rose into two arches held down only by the post. The rain poured in slantways, bathing her face. From behind them, Touhy walked down the plank into the pit in his drenched shirt, the glow of the phone in his hand, shouting above the rain: I have Dublin on the line. Dublin wants to talk to you.

Then Touhy went quiet and stood in the circle. Robert let go and the bulb swung back and forth across the ground. They stared under the creaking wire as the brown and mute bones of the Young Irelander moved in and out of the dark.

GLASS

WHEN I WAS YOUNG I thought my mother was a loose woman. I think it was because of what happened to my dad. He was killed working on a dark morning in February while digging a trench for underground phone cables. A car veered onto the hard shoulder, catapulting him into the air, and after that happened I stopped talking for a while. My mother cried for a week. To make up for my silence, she said.

Another week went by and three more and the silence stayed nested in my mouth. I followed my mother's hand into a creamy building with greenish tiles in it. A man talked to her and then to me and then to her. Might take months or weeks or tomorrow, he said. I wanted to talk but the words couldn't come out, as if blocked by a door or a table or something. Then my mother said she had to get something and left me alone with the professional man.

And now, Paul—your name is Paul, isn't it?

I swung my legs. His tweed jacket smelt of cigarettes. He had more questions.

Think of words as little breaths of air. You can breathe, can't you? Breathe for me, Paul. Let's try it together. He stood up and exaggerated a big breath, pulling his shoulders back, letting it out in a long sigh as he slipped his brown fingertips inside his pockets. He did this for some time. I looked past him to the lawn outside his window where a cloud froze in the blue sky. I thought my words could just as easily be spit too. Then I could spit on him. When my mother came back she asked me to wait outside and then she brought me home and didn't say a word the entire way.

She took a part-time job in the local pub so that she could get out of the house, and, I think now, away from me. We lived in Moycullen, and the pub in the town served tourists, mostly Germans and Americans who stopped for sandwiches and tea on their way to the Connemara mountains or salmon fishing on the Corrib river. It was at this time I thought she was loose for seeing another man, because that's when she met John.

Mr. John Higgins made up for what I could not say. He made up for my silence right from the first day he appeared at the house and shook my hand: I was fourteen, it was 1974. My mother told me that he worked as a signals man at the railway station in Galway City. He visited our house twice a week after that, driving late in the evenings in his Escort after the last train he had to service came in from Dublin, his jacket shoved up around his neck, the distant mountains framing him as he took the last steps to our door and knocked. It didn't take me long to dislike him, and I disliked him all the way through spring and all the way through summer in that big silence the professional man could not penetrate with his tricks. Higgins never stopped talking.

He was loud and twitchy. He fed cigarettes into his mouth for quick puffs, and he was everywhere in the house at the same time, darting from the living room to the kitchen for coffee, to the front door if someone knocked, to the toilet, where he talked to himself. He sucked up all the space around him. My mother wandered around the house whispering like a ghost; I often wondered if she knew he was there.

Sometimes they went out for dinner and a local big band, and when they got back to the bungalow I'd hear them knock over the pots and plates and laugh. I could see them too, if my bedroom door was open, touching each other.

Put on Mr. Sinatra, Carmel. I love Frank, I do, John said.

He took her hand and twirled, his green scarf flowing off his shoulder.

He said, I sang at the Skeffington last week for my brother's birthday. He said I sounded like Tom Jones.

You do in a way, my mother said, and sipped from her whiskey before hugging him with her free hand. He swung away from her, loosened his shirt and winced a song into a pretend microphone.

The summer wind.

And she laughed. John made her laugh.

One night they came back and moved the furniture so that the floor was clear for another dancing session. John set two Brendan Boyer singles to repeat on the turntable and they jived. He grabbed the ribbon from her hair and ran behind the couch, waving it above his head. She ran after him, shouting, Give it back!

Try taking it from me. Go on!

I spent a fortune on that ribbon, she said, leaning across the sofa, stretching her fingers as her figure pressed against the cotton of her dress.

Sixpence if it was a penny, John laughed.

More than that! She giggled and fell limply against him, and he held her straight although I could see that she didn't need the support at all.

Then they played slow music. Then they sat on the couch and he put his arm around her.

You're a fine girl, alright. His sweat glistened across his smile, his white shirt wet from the armpits.

He kissed her cheek, but my mother turned her lips to his. He stroked her hair and she lay back, pulling him down onto her. I lay in bed, the pillow pressed to my ear even though I couldn't shut anything out.

Next weekend, another night of dancing and drinking. They stumbled into the house, chattering wildly at the tail end of some topic. This time John did all the singing and my mother twined red and yellow ribbons through her hair. Then she asked him to turn off the music. He lifted the needle and extinguished the melody.

I want to tell you something, John.

Yeah, oh yeah?

I want to get married again.

Without moving, he placed the needle back to the vinyl and started to sing even before the music started.

I'm serious, she shouted into the noise.

We barely know each other yet, he said.

Will you turn that down?

I need my space, he shouted back. I'm not ready, Carmel. Aren't we having fun? Don't you like me? He danced to her in little dips of his knees, trying to grab her hand.

She turned away, folded her arms. Will you turn that off?

He shook his head, laughing, dancing, singing into his fist.

I'm not going to take that away from you, she said. I just want to have you around enough that we can get used to each other.

He moved around her, trying to get her to swing with him. He turned the music up. She snapped.

Get out, she screamed. Get out, get out!

Even with the record in the background, I shook.

Carmel, I'm only—

Just get out.

He took his jacket and left in the dead of night. She cried herself to sleep while the record turned under the needle. A few days passed and he reappeared, and it started all over again. Music, drinking, arguing. I was angry to hear him refuse her, glad that he did.

My mother knew that I had heard them arguing.

He has a problem with drinking, I think, she said. You should be more forgiving, Paul. I know you don't like him. He needs time. When are you going to say something to me. Just to me?

I wanted to talk to her even less now. Soon her wrists started to swell and she had to give up her part-time job, and her outings fell to a night or two a week at bingo. She took pills she didn't think I saw, the ones she kept hidden with the wine bottles she didn't think I saw. Her eyes darkened and grew hollows, and her hair was a pegged-up bunch of gray. She looked a hundred years older than thirty-four.

As I lay on my bed listening to my mother and her new flame dance and then fight, I wished that my dad would come back for a visit and, with the strong arms that held me as a child, beat the tar out of John Higgins, beat him all the way back to Galway City, call him a waster, and kick his arse a few times more after that. I wanted this even if it meant my father would have to return to his grave at such a late hour. And when the furniture started moving to the edges of the room and the couple pounded the floor with their shoes, I wanted my ancestors to stir from the ground and join my father. I wanted the earliest traces of our family to move from the ground of the Russian Steppes or the Spanish south and give the dancemaster, Mr. Higgins, Esq., the drubbing of the century until all that was left of him was a whimper. I played out the scene like a film I'd watch in the Town Hall cinema: after taking care of Mr. Higgins, my father returns to the house and has tea with my mother and me, tells us how he feels and where he is, and I ask if he knows whether we'll all be together again since he has the inside track now that he's in the afterlife. My dad listens, scratching his chin, which he does when he's thinking but can't find the words. I imagined our conversation: 'Dad, give me a sign that you can see me,' and he says that yes he will, 'You'll see.' And on those dark nights I fell asleep playing that scene over and over and woke up to a world made of only my mother and me, a world that limped on without him, wearing its bravest face.

The summer slipped by, the leaves stiffened and disintegrated, and by mid-autumn John had lost his job as signals man. His manager told him they were cutting back on the Dublin-Galway service until the spring. John started drinking and lost his car to the bank; so now he cycled out to the house evenings, his scarf blowing, his light a needle in the long road.

He and my mother spent more time together, and soon they were arguing again into the night hours. She said she was tired of asking him to move in, and he said she was only asking out of pity now because he'd lost his job. Pity or not, John Higgins soon began leaning his bicycle against the wall of the house earlier most days, letting himself in with an 'I'm back!' and putting his six-pack and sandwich in the fridge. My mother never said anything to him about it, even when she came back from a long walk and found him sleeping on the couch. Then he stopped bringing anything and helped himself to what we had, watching television with his right leg hopping. I never acknowledged him. One day I walked though the living room and he turned to follow me with a stare from his dark face, his lips set, and his fingers tight around a beer.

If you're this angry now, what will you be like when you're my age? he said.

I stopped, unsure whether to keep going or turn around. He leaned forward and poked a finger at me.

Take it easy and don't be so morose all the time. Life is living for the day, Corpus Deum, that's what I say.

I decided that I could not wait for my father to come back from the grave for Christmas. I'd have to do Higgins in myself. He stood up, furious that I didn't respond.

Talk, can't you? Open your bloody mouth and say something, you little git. You make me nervous, like I'm never alone. He shouted now, his whole body spastic.

Go out and play. Go on!

He put the bottle down and took a step toward me. I left quickly, kicked a stone around the yard, then beat it high into the air with a stick.

At the end of November my mother sat me down and told me that I wouldn't be seeing John again.

I hope you're not disappointed, Paul, she said. I like him, but John's afraid of me. You'll understand when you're older.

She laughed and caressed my hair, and I pulled back a little, embarrassed at her affection. We had never been a close family; my father had been a quiet, somewhat lonely man, and I was not used to her touch, even though she was a kind woman. As winter came and deepened, John faded from my thoughts. He is the type who slips easily out of memory, and only his shrill talk or a vinyl record can bring him back now.

An Arctic winter spell comes once every few years to Ireland. The weekend forecast for the middle of December was for heavy snow. By late Thursday, clouds hung over the town.

I lay under a woolen blanket dotted with red donkeys. We were saving oil. The cold made my feet feel like blocks. I had taken off my trousers and draped them around my head for warmth. As I tried to sleep I saw the snowflakes twisting under the street lamp and over a deep frost serrated across the window. After an hour lying in bed I was still shivering.

My mother closed her bedroom door. I squeezed my eyes shut until colors lit up my eyelids. One by one the house lights went off in our neighborhood. At one o'clock it seemed I was the only person awake in the whole town as the snow flung itself against the window, piling onto the sill. I rolled over but couldn't relax. My ear sank against the pillow and I heard the blood roar inside me.

A shadow slapped the bright reflection of the street lamp off my face for an instant. I kicked off the covers and ran to the glass, rubbing a circle in the frozen film with my breath. A machine moved under my window. I cupped my hand and peered as the outline went by, gouging out an arc of snow. The JCB with a plough on the front passed under the street lamp and then into the black, waving its white shawl across the silence between light and dark. The cabin glass made the driver look like an insect in biology class at school.

Morning came and the sun was a pale yellow circle pressed like a fingertip against the ice on the bedroom window. I glanced at the road and saw where the machine had cleared a line for cars. My mother was reading the newspaper at the breakfast table.

Richard and Stephen are coming tomorrow for a few days, she said at the sound of my footsteps. They'll have to stay in your room.

I had met them before. They were her sister's two sons. My mother watched me pour my tea and smiled. Their mother and father need some time alone. Make your room tidy, would you?

I guessed the boys' parents were fighting. I hadn't seen Richard and Stephen in years; they were a year and two younger than I, and that's most of what I remembered about them. But other matters occupied us that day. By eleven o'clock the snow was falling so hard that forecasters called it the heaviest snowfall in Ireland since the Second World War. The lake beside our house froze, and that night's weather was the worst on record, though we weren't as badly hit as the rest of the country. The army trucks moved out of their barracks in the midlands where drifts buried the roads in some of the smaller towns. Up north, gale-force winds cut off outlying islands.

By the time the two boys arrived next day on the early afternoon train and took the bus out to Moycullen, the storm had blown itself out. After they had rested for a couple of hours, we traipsed across the frozen lake since the sky was clearing. It must have been well after six in the evening when the moon floated from a patch of cloud, bright at the edges, its yellow gauze spread across the white ice like butter. I careened on the bike over the ice as the other two stepped cautiously.

My mother called, Remember, the lake is still dangerous even if it's shallow!

Okay, they said, and moved even slower. I cycled off into the middle of the ice and ignored them. A while later, I noticed the brothers gathered about, looking down at the ice. I cycled over.

Jesus, we thought you'd never come, Richard said, and he pointed at something. I let the bike drop and joined them.

There's someone in the ice, Stephen said. Someone's in the ice.

I knelt down, but clouds covered the moon. We waited in the pitch dark until the moon moved out into the stars again and lit up a face that stared at us from under the ice.

Jesus, Richard said.

My nose touched the cold sheet. A boy, maybe seventeen, dressed in a tuxedo, his hands raised to his shoulders, palms facing us, leaning against the dirty glass, as if asking us to let him in, to let him back. His face shone handsome and clear.

We'd better call the police, Stephen said.

I nodded, aware of how calm the lads were and of a strange calm in me, and I thought that maybe they'd seen things at home that might have seemed worse to them. I motioned with digging actions that we could cut the ice and drag him clear.

No, you idiot, said Richard. We'll fall in ourselves.

They skidded back to the house, but I waited with the boy. I brought my face close to his until all that separated our skins was the ice. I put my hands to match his and felt them stick to the surface.

He was silent too.

After Richard and Stephen reached the house my mother ran to the edge of the lake, screaming at me, her words garbled. I left my bike beside the drowned boy in the tuxedo and ran to her. She grabbed me as if from a raging river, hugged me too tightly and too long.

The police came in black coats filled with pencils and notebooks, and they told my mother the boy went missing after a party Thursday night. He was last seen running off with a champagne bottle, they said, shouting something about swimming in the lake. My mother wept into a hanky as she poured the policemen their tea. The poor boy, she kept saying. His poor mother.

In the living room the television said more weather was on the way, and snow was falling again as we went to bed. Richard wanted to sleep on the floor even though it was too cold and hard for him. Stephen fell asleep as soon as I had put out the light; I lay beside him as the moon swung around the roof, thinking about everything and nothing. I knew my mother was worried by everything. It's as if the world had heaped its concerns on her forehead. I slept until the beating of an engine pulled me from the bed and to the window. Two large wheels rotated into the glare of the street light, followed by a short steel frame from which snow blew in a curving wave of dirty white crystals. I looked for a driver but saw only the shape of the JCB and its solitary play against the yellow of the streetlights as it cleared the snowdrifts and mumbled away into the distance. I thought of my father. I wished I knew why he had left without warning and where in the big night he was now, and if he was as alone as the man in the machine or the fellow under the ice. I had once dreamt I met him on a street: we faced each other, trying to talk, but neither of us could get a word past what seemed like glass between us.

I leaned my head against the window and sleep drifted against my forehead.

A noise outside the window woke me to more snow. Then there it was: a shape flitted past the window up to the roof. I looked around: the brothers were buried in their blankets.

Wake up, I said. But the words hadn't a sound to them.

Richard shouted in fright when I shook his shoulder. He twisted into a sitting position.

Wake up, I said. We're going outside. Nothing.

Jesus, you're trying to talk, he said.

Stephen was breathless. Paul is almost talking again. It's a bloody miracle!

Are you both deaf? I said. I spoke silence. I'd surely never speak again.

Richard looked at me with his mouth hung open as he dragged his trousers along the floor and up his legs.

I said, I heard a noise outside, and I pointed to the window because that's all I could do.

Stephen wrapped his scarf tight around his neck and clapped me on the back.

Good man! You lost your voice and now you'll find it. Keep looking!

We crept in single file past my mother's room and the drone of her television to the top of the staircase. The television clicked off, boards creaked across her room, and my mother waltzed to the bathroom a couple of inches from where we crouched. She sang to herself, and the smell of drink harmonized the tune on her breath.

We tiptoed down the stairs and out the front door into the bone cold air. Stephen's red hair flew around his orange cashmere scarf. We tried to run to the pavement, but our steps sank knee-high. We beat our chests for warmth.

I motioned for them to stand still.

A timid voice floated from the roof, a voice I recognized. I wasn't surprised. In recent weeks, word had it that things had not gone well for John Higgins. Word of trouble with another woman and her husband, and Higgins having to leave town for a month to let things settle.

I said, I know who you are. And I heard my words float onto the crisp air.

One side of my face was absent from numbness. We all moved together, our eyes fixed to the figure on the roof, our shoulders touching. I stared until I swayed. Richard and Stephen were probably too interested in the stranger to realize that I had just said something. The mound of snow perched on the roof seemed to oscillate, and an arm lifted a bottle to the head. A chunk of snow fell from his forehead.

Can you get down? Richard said.

I watched the bottle fall with a thud into the snow. I thought how much John could see from the roof: the lake, the fields stretched ghost-white to the sea, the lighthouse.

He grunted and caught hold of the drainpipe. I couldn't tell if he'd heard me. He kicked at the wall of the house, probably trying to get the blood flowing in his legs before shimmying down.

Stephen turned to me. If we climb up to help him, we'll hang by our arms until we freeze too. They'll have to cut us down like cardboard.

The light went on in my mother's bedroom. The window opened and she leaned out. She looked at John as he swayed to her right. Then she looked down at us and back to him and called in a clear voice:

You'll have to let go, John. Go on. Push yourself away from the wall and let go.

I can't.

Push yourself off the wall, John.

I can't stop drinking. I love you, Carmel.

I know, John. Let go of the pipe.

I'm letting go, Carmel.

John fell awkwardly. We struggled through the snow to him.

He's puking, Stephen said.

We dragged him into the house by the shoulders and positioned him on the couch while my mother scurried about in the bright kitchen making chicken soup. Richard took off John's shoes and socks while I undid the shirt. The smell of whiskey was cold on John's lips. Stephen started a fire with wet logs. He crouched down and blew until a flame crept around the sizzling timber.

I helped my mother pour the soup. She looked at me.

Don't be angry with him, Paul. He's lonely, but I won't waste any more time on him, if that's what worries you.

I'm not worried.

She gasped. You're talking again! Oh Paul! She hugged me, her chest heaving.

I heard a noise outside, I said.

It must have been the fright, then. Thank God for that. Thank God for John Higgins. My little boy has found his voice!

After Higgins fell asleep and the two boys went to bed, I made her a cup of tea in the kitchen. She talked and talked about me talking. Then she took a small mirror from her purse and traced the lines on her forehead with a fingertip. She met my gaze unflinchingly.

I'm not getting any younger, don't you see? But a lot of men would like to meet a widow who lives in a clean house. I'm going back to that pub. I'm going to meet a nice man on his holidays. I miss your father, Paul. But I'm lonely. And now you're better. Now I can be better too.

I nodded. I had never heard her use that word, *widow*, as if my talking had loosened a truth in her that spoke to her, finally told her she was alone. I returned to my room, undressed, turned out the light, and listened to the silent white storm heave against the window.

ANOTHER LIFE

ON THE DAY OF HER TRIP to Dublin, Mrs. Mary Connolly took the bus from Listowel to Tralee and the train from there to Heuston Station. When she got off the bus at O'Connell Street she moved steadily in the Friday crowds until she reached the address that matched the one on the envelope. She took her time on the stairs, a handbag in her left hand and banister in her right, feeling with every second step a pressure on the knee, the pain much worse from traveling. The secretary rose and guided her into the office where Mr. Kenny the solicitor looked up from his desk, placed his hands together as if pressing something inside them, and tilted his head.

And to meet you again under these circumstances. He crossed the waxed oak floor and shook her hand. I'm so sorry for your loss.

Mrs. Connolly's answer was lost in her breath. He guided her to the armchair and brought her a glass of water, holding it to her fingertips: everything in his precise movements told her he did not have much time for her that day. He worked on an important street, and Mrs. Connolly doubted very much that she was anything but a break from more important matters, especially near the end of the year. The walls of the office were made of red and brown leather books with gold lettering, the air drenched in the smoke of a recent pipe. It was a day trip for her. In three hours she would be sitting in the train again on the long way back to the south, watching the towns pass, the green life of cows and sheep invisible from the windows of any house.

He stepped back and waited for her to sip the water.

Take that now and you'll feel better.

This was the first time she'd met her husband's solicitor, and she wondered why Mr. Kenny spoke to her as though she were touched with the light brain of age. Either that or he was a very sincere man. That was probably what he was. She watched him return to the folder at his desk and place both hands flat on it.

The life of a man, he said, simply cannot be contained in documents. And such a good man.

That he was, Mrs. Connolly said.

Five weeks before, at the age of sixty-two, Paul Connolly died at home from a heart attack that closed his eyes and killed him as they closed. They had been married for thirty-one years. She had not begun to miss him because she did not understand how he could be gone without notice, and she expected to see him around every corner, to meet him again as suddenly as she lost him. Wills divide property, and the law says little about companionship: that was the business of the funeral mass and those who spoke from the lectern, friends who missed him and conducted themselves with fraught composure. She remembered sitting in the front row, thinking that poems and prayers must exist because they said what emotions born with weak voices could not utter, except in the strongest. Mary did not feel she was one of those.

Mr. Kenny uncapped a fountain pen with one hand and slid the pages from the folder to her with the other.

I need your signature in three places as indicated, he said.

She placed her glass on the desk and her signature on the pages without reading anything, since her husband had been a careful man and would not have hired a careless solicitor for all these years. Her name shook on the page, and some letters in the middle of her name dipped under the line as the pen scratched across the silence.

Mr. Kenny examined each of the signed sheets and slipped them back into the folder.

And now, he said, the Last Will and Testament. This can be a difficult time—he smiled and interlaced his fingers—and if you wish, I can dispense with the formal reading and point out the salient features.

That would be fine.

Very well then, in summary—

I meant fine to read it, she said. It's fine for you to read the whole letter he wrote.

Mr. Kenny nodded. I'm so sorry.

He pressed the button on a box. Nora, I'll be running ten minutes late. When Mr. Stephens comes, have him wait and offer him something.

As Mr. Kenny read the will, Mrs. Connolly leaned forward with her eyes closed. These were now the last words of her husband's she would ever hear, and the language, though legal, felt like a poem to her read at a memorial service, the wishes of this man she loved and for such a long time translated into the language of the courts: Monies will be deposited from the estate . . . and all the contents thereof.

Mr. Kenny had said on the phone that she could sign all the forms in Listowel, but this was why she came to Dublin, to hear these words, not read them alone under the desk lamp in their house. She leaned back quietly in the red leather armchair—it was huge and she was not—as she did not want to be distracting Mr. Kenny as he read. The will was a year old, dated six months after Paul retired. And now to hear him survive in it, his voice in the bank accounts, the house, his pension.

In the list of assets, Mr. Kenny listed an address she did not remember: 5 Castle Close, Oranmore, in the County of Galway. He continued to read, his eyes like a zip that ran along the sentences and opened their contents to 'and all the contents thereof.' Five paragraphs later it was done.

He said, There it is, Mrs. Connolly. I expect no challenges, and the legal process will continue to a smooth conclusion. He closed the folder and handed her an envelope. Here are some other documents: keys and so forth.

Mrs. Connolly said, Thank you.

He immediately stood and glanced at the door behind which no doubt Mr. Stephens was at that moment waiting for the advice, the resolution, the balm for the worry that produced him in person at these offices. She thought to mention that she did not remember that address, but if it were anything other than an asset on paper, a tax address, Mr. Kenny would have said something. She did not want to keep Mr. Stephens waiting and shook Mr. Kenny's hand even as he glanced over her shoulder again.

* * *

At 3:53 on Friday afternoon Mary Connolly walked down the steps from the solicitor's offices and reached the light of the street and turned right. Her right leg sharpened the limp in the twenty-minute walk to the bus stop for the station. In her hand she held the key that Paul had given to his friend Mr. Kenny, as well as the deed and insurance papers. A tax address does not have a key. All the way to Tralee in the train she felt the key in her coat pocket, what she didn't know getting bigger inside her with worry until it became the weight of a house. She found some distraction in the view, but the trip was long because she had not thought to bring anything to read. She took the last bus to Listowel and crossed the road in the dark to the Listowel Arms Hotel, where at the corner table in the lounge she ordered tea and biscuits as the bar filled with the night crowd. When she felt able, she walked the ten minutes home, clutching her coat and the plastic brown handbag with one hand as she let herself in. The cat's tail flowing between the chairs and the table in the dining room eventually produced the rest of the cat. It trotted along the red strip of carpet to the bowl in the dark kitchen where it pawed the floor, because it knew that this movement always somehow produced a tin of food.

Mary went to Paul's car and found the map of Ireland folded in the glove box. She spread it on the living-room table under the light and carefully secured her glasses until her finger traced the roads from Listowel to Limerick and past Ennis and on to Galway—there it was, Oranmore, five miles southeast of the city, a long way from Listowel, five hours. She left the silver key on the lines and circles and went to the couch in her coat and shoes. The cat soon followed and settled its few pounds down onto the folds of her lap.

The couch was in the extension Paul had built a couple of years ago: a glasshouse, or rather a glass-covered patio at the side of the house, with plants and a terracotta tile-covered floor. Mrs. Connolly looked to the dark sky through the glass frames.

Paul, what did you do?

Mrs. Connolly rested for the weekend. The journey, particularly walking in crowded Dublin, exhausted her. At eight o'clock on Monday morning, Mrs. Sachdeva from next door brought over vegetables and curry in a plastic bag the cat sniffed. Her husband was a doctor in the hospital, and the Indian couple had drawn closer to Mary after Paul's death.

Feed her anything she likes, Mrs. Connolly said. She knows what she likes, she'll tell you. I'll be gone for three days at the most. It'll be a treat for her.

Mrs. Sachdeva nodded. Don't you worry, Mrs. Connolly. I will come morning and evening. She held out the foil in which the meal was packed. Now this is for you, not the cat. It's the vegetables you like. My husband says to call him from Galway if you feel ill, and he will come to you.

Thank you, Mrs. Connolly said. The doctor had already given her something for sleep, but the pills were still in the kitchen drawer. She was managing a few hours a night.

At twenty minutes past eight she went to the garage with one small bag and started up the green and brown 1963 Morris Minor. Paul kept it in excellent order, his love and his joy. She'd driven the car twice in the past two months, both times to the post office in the rain. And now for the second time in as many days she was engaged on a trip that would take her farther than she had traveled on her own in decades.

She reversed out the driveway and turned onto a bigger street and out of town, proceeding at the legal speed with both hands sloped over the wheel, and wearing her reading glasses to see the road signs better, which did not help. She had learned the names of towns on the way so she could stop to ask if she got lost, and she repeated them to herself to keep the list in her head: Limerick, Ennis, Oranmore, the same way she remembered things to buy in the shop. She pulled the scarf down both sides of her face to block out distractions. Soon a line of cars rode their brakes behind her, but the road was too narrow for her to let them pass, turn after turn, until a hard shoulder opened and she pulled to the side, where she saw that the speed limit was 100 kilometers an hour, not 60.

The wind buffeted the Morris as she neared the estuary of the Shannon river. She wore the same brown dress and shoes and coat she wore to Dublin. Mary did not have a large wardrobe, and the bag contained a cardigan for the evening and her heart medicine and odds and ends for a trip like this.

Paul worked as a journalist, first in Athlone for twenty years, and when they moved to Listowel he had enough of a reputation to work freelance, covering the arts and occasionally politics in the southeast and west, which brought him on frequent trips along the coast for a day or two at a time. It was the life he loved, meeting people, attending concerts, wine receptions in the suit he draped from the coat hanger in the back of the Morris as he took off for another interview or festival. His other passion was black-and-white photography, and many of the photos that accompanied his articles in the national newspapers were his, and the camera and the tripod went with him. Although a contented man, Paul was especially happy on the mornings or evenings he drove away on an assignment.

She never went with him because the life she loved was keeping the house and reading, helping with some events in the town every now and then. Her life was simpler from the start and she never overcame it, the urge that living should be a variation on the same pattern. The same simplicity leaked into her clothes, her manner of speaking, the books she read, mostly romance: she owned stacks of novels by excellent writers who had chosen to write on a theme and stick with it. She lived that other exotic life in the pages of her books and wondered, after she pulled up her nylon stockings and made another cup of tea, what she would do if she found herself on a Caribbean island in the arms of a tall stranger, a man of means and a mysterious past. She would be lost on an island with a man other than Paul.

Their life had been a simple one, quiet and without children, and she often regretted that a child had not come into their lives. In the Ireland of the sixties they were too embarrassed to go beyond mentioning it to the doctor, to ask if anything might be done. She often gave a shape and a name and a place in her heart to this baby who never arrived, as Paul must have, this silent presence who never spoke and for that reason was the loudest thing in their lives. But time passed and the child looking for birth inside her grew quieter, and when she had reached an age when that was no longer possible, the child she hoped for went away.

South of Galway she took the coast road and came to Oranmore. She stopped for a snack in a café and showed the waitress the address.

Oh yes, that's one of the new developments. She pointed out the window. Over that way.

The girl was pretty, said she was from Poland, and Mary told her how good her English was and stared out at the street and at the roofs of the buildings opposite. The girl drew a map on the paper menu because she said that Mary looked lost.

Mary drove two rights, two lefts, and another right until she came to the sign *Castle Close*. On the left skyline was the top of the castle on the bay, and on the right, two rows of facing houses and gardens, a well-kept and prosperous street. Three children rode bikes and a dog ran the path with a stick in its mouth. The early afternoon sun and the salt from the wind mixed with the smell of dinners. She let the car idle at the corner and found her hands trembling. The Morris chugged as she stared ahead, afraid to look left or right, lest her eyes fall on a house she knew was his even though she didn't see the number. She felt him near. He could be in the car, sitting where she was, having turned into the street with his tuxedo and camera and his bag, and now driving along slowly, seconds from the house at the end of his journey, but it was she who drew up to Number 5 and saw that it looked just like Number 6 and Number 4. She waited a minute in the car, closed her eyes. Whatever she might see in that house, she thought, would not change any of the life they owned together, would not diminish it. She stood onto the road and walked up the driveway and placed the key into the lock and turned it. The door slid open easily, and Mary Connolly stepped into a hallway, feeling small as the daylight cast her shadow ahead into the kitchen at the end of the hall, a long shadow entering before her.

The hall floor was wooden, and large palm trees in pots that did not look withered lined the wall: they should have shown traces by now. To her right as she walked was a line of photos at eye level on light green paint. A photograph is dated instantly by color, she once heard Paul say. But black and white is timeless.

The first was Paul with a group she did not know, he was in his good suit and holding a drink. A woman in her late thirties stood behind Paul, looking at him and not the camera. Two photos to the left, the same woman in the background, among other people but still looking at Paul. He looked different in the photographs, more outgoing. That young woman must have been part of the society Paul found here, people in the arts.

She could not move from the spot, seized at the heart by this face she knew so well, the silver hair, the light tan, the high forehead, the eyes that had lived and had room for more. He looked happy. Now she was looking at him from the place he stood when he must have hung these photographs. In the silence of this hallway, in the cold late afternoon, there was no romance, only the stab of his being lost to her all new again.

The hall opened into a living room, the large fireplace of brown stone with logs arranged in the grate and paper and twigs stuffed underneath ready to be lit, the candles on the mantelpiece, a couch that faced the fireplace and a coffee table with magazines: photographic glossies, Galway society, travel clubs. The kitchen led to a rear garden: an antique stained-glass window hanging from ceiling chains to cover the French doors. She went behind it and saw the deck with the table and chairs, the fountain and the shed, a bicycle at the side wall. The house had far less furniture than their own, and more light except for the living room, which was open on both sides to the hall and the kitchen. In the cupboards she found things she knew Paul liked: Jacob's cream crackers, Old Time Irish marmalade, two Cuban cigars and the long matches to light them, a washed ashtray. No crumbs, no bread gone stale, no bad milk in the fridge. Paul liked to have things in order.

Habits are portable. In the kitchen Mary cleaned the counter and ran water over the cloth and draped it over the middle section. She would have loved to light the fire in the living room but could not warm herself to those flames he meant for himself. She did not want to eat Paul's food, preferring instead to leave the jars and packets in the shape his hands left them. She turned the gas knob under the kettle, and not wanting to move the kitchen chairs, stood while drinking the tea. Then she washed and dried the mug. The downstairs toilet was dark and smelled of lavender.

At the bottom of the stairs she looked up at the beige carpet that led to the landing, a bedroom up there, no doubt. Mary took the steps, leaning heavily on her good knee. She was out of breath by the time she reached the darkness of the first floor and opened the door of the bathroom: a shade covered the window and she felt the wall for a switch but found none. Instead she turned on the landing light and saw her reflection in the cabinet mirror move aside as she opened it to a toothbrush in a green plastic cup, still white with toothpaste, and another cup beside the bathtub filled nearly to the top with black tea: he had died in the bath at home in Listowel, and here she touched the cup he forgot to put away and felt the cold china fill her; she placed her finger in the cold tea, the next person to touch it after him. From the sink she took the brush, the silver fine hairs curled in it, and across the hall in the large cupboard opposite, she found shoes and socks and shirts and jacket, and in the bottom drawer, his underpants.

This was the man. She held the underpants in her hands, remembered their quiet undressing in the dark even when they were younger. She held the white shirt to her face and breathed in, he was lying beside her now and turning to her in his sleep, and she watched him before sleeping, that comfort she felt with him. These were clothes she had not seen before. She held up the loose shirt that no longer contained a body: the detergent had not fully masked the smell of Paul's skin, the honey smell.

She felt the handle of the bedroom in the dark and imagined what lay beyond that door, the shape of his head in a pillow, the last traces of a living man left long after the last traces of the dead have been put away. Beyond that door, she wondered what books were arranged on the bedside table she was sure he must have put there to help him sleep. What he saw when he looked out the window.

At half past two in the afternoon she pressed the cold metal and opened the door. She saw the baby.

A dream formed around the next minutes that somehow brought her out of the house. The dream left the front door open behind her and curled up with her in the back seat of the Morris on the street, where the wind smeared the windows with rain off the bay and rocked the car gently as the day disappeared from the cold street, the same street Paul saw from the bedroom. Soon the temperature in the car matched the weather outside, and the draughts ran her skin cold. She hugged the coat about her, listening to the street-lights clank overhead in the wind and counting now the times he had gone on trips overnight. She lay on her side and shook, watching the windows. The car was the only place she felt safe, Paul's old car.

Early in their lives together, Mary sensed his restlessness. When they moved to Listowel from Athlone, she quietly hoped it might bring him a life he wanted. He loved the annual writers' week and camped out at the Listowel Arms. The friends he found were literate and intellectual. He brought three of them over to the house every week for social evenings in the living room, and he was happiest on those nights. Mary, because she felt she did not have the learning to keep up with them, preferred to read her paperbacks in the extension.

Jack, a retired civil servant in his seventies, drove to the get-togethers in a Blue Vauxhall from his house in Tralee. He wore a shirt and tie under his coiffed white beard stained with tobacco and brought records of Roslyn Tureck playing Bach. Siobhan, the most opinionated of the group, was a widow in her fifties and attractive. She was in her sixth year of a doctorate in psychology at the university in Cork. Joe, the youngest, wore a mop of black hair and a loose tweed jacket. He was a journalist and the quiet one, content to hang his head and listen and nod.

At the service, Jack read perfectly from a famous European novel; Joe stuttered, trying to put memories in order, laughing and breaking down until he had to leave the lectern; Siobhan looked everywhere except at Mary as she described Paul Connolly's adventurous and artistic mind and his willingness to break intellectual and societal molds. Mary did not hear much of what they said. She was busy looking at Paul's coffin, thinking that his death was a condition from which he would recover and return to her. When the mass ended, Siobhan said to her as if into a great distance: I'm sorry for your loss. She did not come to the house afterwards, and once the funeral was over, Mary saw no more of the group. Jack, Siobhan and Joe were Paul's friends, after all. Paul was the one they came to see.

Mary opened her eyes in the Morris, still on her side, and the pain woke with her, matching any movement inch for inch. Her leg had dropped into the space between the back and front seats and gone stiff. The children were playing in the street. A ball hit the gate and a boy's head panted up to the door. Mary stayed down until he ran off. She opened the back door and swung her legs to the path but couldn't get up straight away, just as she often had to wait for the cat to jump off her lap because it didn't get off until it had to, when she was almost standing straight. She let the wrinkled coat fall about her and shut the door.

The boy with the ball shouted across the road: You slept for an hour in the back seat, didn't we see you, and my mother came over too and we all watched you.

Two other boys laughed and they all ran into separate gardens. The wind blew through the thin coat and into the bareness she felt everywhere about her. It was coming up to half past four in the afternoon. She decided to buy some bread in the town because she could not go into the house, and she walked out of the estate and onto the main street in Oranmore. A bakery was still open there.

What can I do for you, the man with the beard and glasses said.

I was wondering if I could have some bread, Mary said.

The man turned, Now what kind of bread? The wheat, the white, the sourdough, and then I'll need to know if you want a half baguette or the full one. He coughed into his white sleeve.

I'll have that one, Mary said. No, the next one, the well-baked one over there. She kept pointing. The next one, she said. There.

Ah, the half baguette of white French bread.

When she paid him, the baker sifted money in the till. Are you visiting?

My husband had a house here.

Really, he said. And who is your husband?

Paul Connolly.

The man looked distantly into the small chambers of the till. I can't say I've met him.

Mary said, White hair, a tan, in his early fifties, a handsome man.

You mean the man with the camera?

Yes, that's him.

The baker looked puzzled and went polite. But of course, yes, here every couple of weeks, a very nice man. Now here's your bread, Mrs. Connolly.

She said, Did you ever talk to him?

The man's head shook before she finished asking. No, he was here very briefly, always knew what he wanted. In and out, that was Paul.

Mary sat by the small table at the window and watched the cars, the shopping bags, the idle business of a Monday in a small western town. The bakery was well lit and warm, but she was cold. The window let her see out and not be outside, be inside and not quite inside. She did not want to leave, and twenty minutes later she walked to the counter again.

A tea, please, and a bun.

This time the baker did not ask her what type of bread or type of bun or size, or what kind of tea and from what part of the world. He poured a cup of tea and put a bun on a plate and handed them to her.

No charge, he said. We're closing in a few minutes and there's no charge for those.

Mary turned and dropped the plate to the ground and the tea out of the cup: it splashed over her coat and her left shoe. She dropped everything and sat heavily on the floor and stared at the wall, but not the bakery wall.

Almost six weeks after his death and the funeral, less than two hours ago, her husband Paul looked at her through the door of the bedroom, and there was no room in Mary to see anything else now. She had seen his eyes. In the large color photograph on the bedroom wall above the headboard, the baby had Paul's blue eyes.

An elderly couple from the corner table shuffled to her in a blur of words.

Are you okay?

Mary said, My husband looked at me.

I didn't do anything, the baker said, coming from behind the counter with a broom.

Now sit up if you can, the woman said. You've had a fall, God love you.

They helped her up and Mary brushed her coat. The

owner swept the floor around her in tight little whisks. I'm
closing now, if you don't mind, he said. Can I get a taxi for
you?

We'll take her home, the woman said.

No, just take me to the house, Mary whispered.

I'll bring the car up to the front, the man said.

The older man said, Where do you live?

Mary tried to remember the address. I can't remember.

She watched the town go by as the couple drove her
around Oranmore in their car. The smell of the bay water,
the clouds, the castle, it all floated by the windows and
seemed made of a substance other than what she could smell
or see. She could never come back.

If you could remember one word from the address, the
man said.

There was a castle in it, Mary said.

Ah, the couple said together. They changed direction,
and soon Mary saw the Morris.

That's it, she said.

The woman touched Mary's arm and asked her to be
careful. After they drove away, Mary got into the back seat
of the Morris with that pain in her knee flaring again.
Perhaps that was where her heart was. The evening drifted
across the houses and the lights came on. The breeze blew
into the open door of 5 Castle Close. She had the cardigan
and the coat at least, and the seat was warm.

She woke before dawn in a parked car on a dark and
empty street. The rain on the windshield delivered her waking thought, that Paul had a child with another woman and
maintained a house that Mary did not know about. She

leaned into her reflection and touched the cold window with her forehead and joined the old woman who lived in that hard, thin, rainy world of glass. Was she that old? He had divided his life in two. Would it have been better to know? She would not have been able to cope at all.

They must have known. The talk on their social evenings sometimes filtered through the walls of her romance novels, and one evening Siobhan's voice rose, calling dishonesty a betrayal of everyone. Paul's voice was softer, something about truth hurting others. Jack's voice alone was normal: the moral life was what everyone wanted, but because their own lives were complicated, they sought it in the lives of others. Nothing as usual from Joe.

The lights of Galway glowed yellow against the night. Mary started the car and in two minutes was driving out of Oranmore, or else she was dreaming it, she felt so far away from the life she knew. This was her life, she had no other.

Three times she stopped the car, twice to cry as the past day caught up with her; when a child she had been like that too, never made a fuss or said anything, and only long after being hurt did she cry. The third time she stared at the cars going by as the wind whipped the folds of her coat. Had she ever known Paul? She felt the rain through her shoes. But there were no new conversations she and Paul could have, she could only replay the old ones.

It was still morning in Listowel. Mary parked the Morris in the garage and unlocked the door of the house. The cat landed on the kitchen floor and ran to her, wound around her ankles, pawed the floor in front of the dish Mrs. Sachdeva had kept full.

You missed me, Mary said.

She saw the light blinking on the telephone and pressed the message button.

A voice hesitated into words: Mary, this is Joe. Please call me when you can. He gave a telephone number and the line clicked.

She replayed the message again, listened to it fill up the house, a friendly voice with a feeling in it that made her feel better. She wrote down the number because she did not have it. Then she called the solicitor in Dublin.

The secretary answered: Good morning, Mr. Kenny's offices.

This is Mary Connolly in Kerry. I'd like to speak to Mr. Kenny.

The silence became Mr. Kenny's voice: I'm afraid I have very little time, Mrs. Connolly.

I won't keep you. I'm back from Galway.

Ah yes.

I did not know about the house. Did you know about the baby?

The silence returned. The offices of silence, Mr. Kenny's offices.

He spoke with as many pauses as words: I presumed he told you. The other party never lived with him, there was a generous lump-sum payment. The other party agreed that your husband had no other obligations and signed legal documents. The other party has no occupancy rights. She is now married I believe.

Mary said, What did Paul tell you about me?

Listen when I tell you this, Mary. In all the years I've known the man, he never uttered a word against you.

A condition, his being dead, from which Paul would recover. This thought returned as Mary stood in the hall holding the phone, looking around her. The cat was the cat. The armchair was the armchair, the couch in the extension, the plants, the books piled on the floor, they were still a couch and plants and books, and if she were gone for a hundred years they would remain so, the reflection she left. She had loved him for so long.

Mr. Kenny said, Do you have other instructions, Mary?

She said, Don't do anything.

I don't understand.

Mary did not have the time to explain it to him.

She imagined what would happen next in the paperbacks: Mary confronts the three friends. Jack pleads ignorance. Siobhan says an astute young woman knew a lonely man when she saw one and lured Paul into the trap. Joe says that maybe Paul felt new in Galway, and among new friends he met this woman and lost himself in the moment, or in many moments. Later in the plot, Siobhan in her white coat and windswept blond hair meets Mary at the gate.

Forgive him? He fooled you, he fooled me too. How can you be so simple?

After Mary left down the phone, she made a cup of tea and walked to the armchair where the cat found her lap and curled into purrs. She picked up the romance novel and opened it on the bookmarked page from weeks before, where she stopped reading at Paul's death: a story of passion and intrigue in the South Pacific. Mary traveled a paragraph and put the book down as the cat grew hotter. The long drive was still driving in her. She was tired, and now she could rest.

The afternoon sky blew in the trees above the roof, rustled the glass of the conservatory and scuttled late leaves across the garden. To forgive, and now. To win all that time from bitterness, where a broken heart might never win back its ease. She did not have the time not to forgive.

Mary slipped down into sleep with a thought of the day to come. It was the story of those novels piled beside her armchair that life is simple in the end, and if the novels were true, it was her life now. So in the morning, after she brushed her hair, made the breakfast and fed the cat, or perhaps in the late part of the morning if she slept, she could walk to the hotel for a cup of tea, and then she was certain she would see what had been true in their lives.

THE SUMMER OF BIRDS

MY MOTHER LEFT THE HOUSE quietly in May when the air was full of new birds that were born out of the trees and the sky in a single day it seemed, even two that hopped along my windowsill every morning and sang. She left when I was at school on the last day of the term, and when I came home my father was standing in the kitchen, still white with cement from the building site where he worked. I knew something was wrong because he was never back at the house this early. When he saw me he poured a cup of tea and put it in front of me.

Your mother is visiting her relatives for a while.

I had heard the silence all spring between them like a balloon so big they couldn't stay in the same house until it went down again.

What is a while? I said.

His hand rested a moment on my shoulder and was gone.

I don't know.

I felt the shake in his hand before he took it away. He went into the living room and read the same newspaper all day. The rest of the same day I spent waiting for her to come back, and later, upstairs in the bedroom, I left crumbs and water out on the windowsill for the birds and waited some more for my mother, but sleep came first.

The next morning the birds woke me when they fluttered against the glass. Their shadows chirped and their heads dipped to the water and seeds as if knitting with them. I ran to the window and they took off, though I didn't worry because they knew where I lived. I looked out at the distant blue line of Galway Bay: from the second floor I could see the mountains rise on the far side and a sea boat trail its white lace to where the open waters of the Atlantic began. Now the summer lay in front of me and felt like a space too big for me to ever fit inside. When my mother returned it would be smaller again and I could play in it. I ran to the top of the stairs and listened for sounds in the house, for the kettle being picked up and water to pour. Normally this early she would be singing to herself or have a song from the radio playing in the kitchen, but from downstairs I heard nothing. She was still gone. In a few minutes I found my father sitting there in front of a cup, and it wasn't even the one he always drank from.

He lifted his head and spoke softly:

I'll stay at home today while we think about who'll take care of you. The neighbors will stop in as well.

I'll be fine, Daddy.

He came over and lifted me up, gave me a squeeze. That's my girl.

I made him another cup of tea and we sat in the kitchen. I knew he had to work a lot because the house was new and we had never had a lot of money, and since my mother would be gone for a few days, it was my turn to do something. I was old enough.

I can take care of myself.

He smiled, I know you can.

We lived in a suburb east of the city, another development of many that spread white houses over the green hills like spilled milk, where a new road appeared out of trees and grass every few months. Ireland was doing well. My father was busy working because it was the same all over the country, he said, new houses going up everywhere, a boom. Even so he stayed at home for a couple of days, and on the morning of the third the phone rang and my father looked at the clock and asked me to answer it instead. I heard her voice at the other end, my mother's, and imagined her holding the phone, the tight wire that brought her voice through the cream telephone. She asked me how I was and told me that she'd be home one of the days—straight away I asked her when that day was, and she said she wasn't sure.

I told her that two birds were at my window in the morning, that they were brown and made a lot of noise. They were probably starlings, she said, or sparrows or thrushes, and they were getting used to the food: they would sing all summer for me now, every morning. When she said goodbye I ran upstairs and searched the sky for them and heard singing, the food had turned into song, and I asked them to keep a lookout for her, since they could see the whole town.

She did not come back the next day. On the fourth night she was gone my father went to the laundry room and came out with a guitar he used to play when I was much younger. It had leaned for years in the corner as the sun crossed the room over the clothes that draped across chairs and in the hampers, and sometimes I smelled the wood when it was warm. I left the door of my bedroom open and listened to him tune the strings. The first strums soon drifted upstairs, slow and with lots of space in between. I did not hear a tune but knew there was one in there somewhere.

When I went downstairs next morning the guitar was still in the living room. He'd even wiped it clean with a cloth. A music book lay open on the armchair.

We had our breakfast, and then he said, In a few days someone will come who can help.

No hurry, Daddy, I said.

I didn't want a new person in the house. We could manage and it was only a few days anyway. Maybe he could explain everything to the people at work and they'd let him stay at home until my mother arrived back. I wondered how long a few days meant. He went into the living room and notes filled the house for the rest of the morning as he bent over the guitar in the armchair. He was a big man, and when he strained to make chord shapes with his left hand his legs tensed and the veins bulged in his forehead as he held his breath before strumming lightly with his right hand.

This is hard, he said when he saw me watching. I used to play when I met your mother. But these hands. He held them up as if they were things he was getting used to.

On the fifth night of my mother's disappearance I arranged the crumbs in a line on the window sill with a cap of water at the end so the birds would find them in the first light, even left the window open in case they wanted to come in and fly around. That meant I had to go under the blankets from the cold, but I still heard the guitar from the living room, the notes my father plucked from the strings and the silences between them as he struggled to make the right shapes on the fretboard. The last thing I remember of that night was when my eyes closed and I saw small foals trying to stand up in a field, not knowing how.

All those new roads brought more than new houses to where I lived. New people too. They appeared one or two at a time, never in groups. One of them turned up in the schoolyard in the months before the summer break and stayed well away from everyone. Then two older ones were seen in the park near the woods. People said they found bags and a shoe by the river, and that if you saw a few of them, that meant many more were hiding; and sure enough, the single ones turned into groups of them coming out at night more often, that's what I thought, and then we heard news that they had even started to come into the pubs and the restaurants

By April there were a lot in plain view moving around the town and especially near the supermarket in the car park, and they were groups now, four and five, each day a little closer, until I heard that if you stopped at all outside the supermarket they would gather at the car, and I heard that when people brushed them away they stepped back, all at once like birds, and some people said that soon the town would be full of them because they were bringing up their young.

On the sixth evening after my mother went away, my father came back to the house with a man called Tommy. Tommy promised to look in on me every now and then because I was alone and everyone agreed that I needed looking after. Tommy came from the pub where my father must have met him. He had a newspaper rolled in his right hand and did not take his coat off as he poured a bottle of stout into a glass. After a few minutes he asked my father to come to the sitting-room window where there was a view of the back of the supermarket and some of the new people, but my father was in the kitchen cooking bacon and didn't hear, so Tommy pointed a finger out the window and shouted: Let them see we're watching. Then he put his finger to his lips for quiet and whispered.

They're out tonight. Do you want to see?

My father spoke from the kitchen, his voice blowing in with the smoke: What?

Come on. Tommy took hold of my shoulder and moved me closer to the window.

I saw two of them like shadows at the end of the street in the concrete yard near the river, and I squirmed out of Tommy's grasp. This must have been the same Tommy my mother said she never wanted in the house.

Don't be afraid, he said. You're safe in here, they can't touch you here.

I'm not afraid, I said.

In the concrete yard two older ones were sitting on a wall. They weren't doing anything. An evening rain shower blew papers across the parking spaces, but the rain didn't seem to matter to them, so I thought a different rain or a worse rain fell where they used to be. I liked the rain too.

My father walked in with the plate and Tommy let go of me and then nodded to the window. They've moved to the end of the street. Won't be long now. Next thing they'll be moving in next door.

You're probably right, my father said, and closed the music book on the table.

On the seventh day after my mother left we were watching a film on the television when Tommy knocked on the front door and let himself in, saying, I'm here!

As he walked into the room I saw a shadow outside because the windows were open with the heat, and they went by, a group of four this time, silent with their heads down, still nothing but fleeting shadows moving along our street and keeping close to the walls. Tommy ran straight to the window and shouted out after them, Go back to your own country.

My father was watching the television and seemed in a different place, chewing with open eyes, still wearing his work boots though he wasn't at work that day.

Tommy turned to me and said, Go on, say it to them, they have to hear it. They've reached your street now, you can't just do nothing. That's how they win.

My father said nothing, and to keep Tommy quiet I said it, told them go back home. They didn't hear me because I whispered it on purpose, but Tommy was still pleased. You're a brave young girl to say something like that. Most people are afraid.

The shadows looked like they didn't want to be in our town either, like they were lost, and I wanted them not to be lost. I pulled away from Tommy, and as the first week of my summer drew to a close I wondered why my mother had been swapped for that man and what he was doing in our house anyway.

My father went back to work. Tommy continued to

drop in at strange times, making himself gradually at home. He was going part-time to the university, taking courses in civilization, he told my father. Even on wet evenings he wore sandals and thick woolen socks that he dried in front of the fire. He crossed his legs as he read the paper, and the smell of his big feet filled the room and the hallway. He always carried a book or a newspaper. Whenever you were saying anything he was drawing in a breath to say something himself. My father said that I should listen to Tommy, that he was studying at the university and was one of very few chosen, out of hundreds, to take special courses on the weekends.

My mother called again on Friday during the day when my father was at work and Tommy was on one of his visits. I went to the hall and closed the door after me so he wouldn't hear. I held the phone close to my ear and listened carefully so that I could measure how far away she was from the sound of her voice along the wires. She asked me if I was taking care of the birds.

I feed them every day, I said. I even know them now, which is the man and which is the woman bird. They come every morning.

Tommy must have heard because I saw the shadow of his sandals move under the living-room door. I wanted to ask my mother when she thought she might be coming back but Tommy's sandals were in the hallway now. She said she had to go and that she would call in two days.

That reminds me of a film, he said.

As I put the phone down, he leaned forward, A famous film, you know, a man called Hitchcock. *The Birds*, there's more and more of them.

I walked around him and into the kitchen. Tommy followed me and said that the film was about what happens if you don't keep count of things: the place gets full of them and they attack you. People's faces torn up and bloody.

He said, I discussed it at the university with one of the professors at lunch.

I sat in the kitchen and waited until he left, sorry that I never got a chance to ask my mother where she was and when she was coming back.

My father came home from work and played the guitar with cement on his hands, the same hands with cuts on them that lugged heavy bags and rocks all day. But the gaps in the notes were getting shorter, the tune was appearing more. I went upstairs without anything for the birds and closed the window and drew the curtains in case they got in during the night and attacked me, because even though I didn't like Tommy, if it happened in the film it must be true. I fell asleep, listening to my father search for the right notes in front of the fire.

The next morning I woke when the birds sang, saw their shapes walking back and forth across the sill, heard their singing in the sunlight, and I wanted to feed them crumbs and put more water into the bottle cap. They might peck me and attack my hands and then my eyes, flood across the room through the open window, and I'd never make it to the bedcovers. The following morning they sang again and their shadows moved right and left, looking for the food. I missed not opening the window and watching the sea in the distance and smelling the salt even here, miles from the coast, but I didn't want to be attacked. They tapped the glass with their beaks and stayed still, waiting for the crumbs. I watched the shadows from behind the blinds until they flew off.

That was the day my mother was due to call, and my father smiled when he saw me watching the minute hand on the clock.

Don't worry, he said. She won't forget.

He was playing the guitar in the living room and I was standing by the phone when I saw Tommy's shadow fill the front door. He walked in.

You're getting better on the guitar, he called out, tapping his newspaper against the wall.

Do you really think so? My father came to the hall.

It was true, he was getting better. I could tell what the song was now, the same one my mother used to sing in the house. He was learning it so she'd hear and remember.

I declare, my father said holding the guitar, I love Waylon Jennings.

Tommy moved past me and went into the living room. Play some national songs, he said. Let's hear some patriot songs.

What ones? I heard my father say as the door closed.

My mother did not call that day as she was supposed to, but I understood why. She knew that Tommy was in the house. When I woke at sunrise something filled the room and it took a minute to hear: it was silence. I looked out through the blinds at just the light. All day long I wondered where the birds could be and why they didn't come, because they had to be hungry.

My father and Tommy drank a lot that day, singing and playing, and I kept to myself. Come nightfall I opened the window and left bread and water.

I'm sorry I didn't feed you, I said as loudly as I dared.
Please come back and I will feed you what I have.

On Monday morning I sneaked out of the house and
walked to the supermarket to buy some sweets, and one of
the shadows followed me. He smiled at me in his school uniform, the maroon tie looped under his strange face, and said
that he was taking extra classes to catch up. I was surprised
that I knew exactly what he was saying. His face broke into
a white smile and he held out his hand, and in it I saw the
red spot with yellow stripes. I knew I should have walked
away, but I didn't. I looked at it. It was one of the sweets I
liked. I saw Tommy in the supermarket too, wearing a white
apron and standing over a box with a pencil in his mouth,
so he must have been very busy, working there and also
going to the university. I think he saw me, but I think I got
away with it. I took the sweet and ran home, and out of my
cupboard I took one of my own sweets.

I ran back to where the boy with the maroon tie was
standing on the street with his mother. I had asked him to
wait for me, and now I went up to them with my hand out.
His eyes grew big around the sweet. His mother told him to
say thank you. I went home with the red one he gave me, the
one with the lemonade taste.

Shortly after five my father called and said he was meeting my mother in the town and did I mind waiting, that
Tommy would come, and he'd asked the people next door to
look in too.

I said, Can you bring her home with you for a while?

I'll ask, he said. I put down the phone and ran up to my
room.

I knew Tommy was in the house when I heard him cough and the fridge door open, then he lit the fire the way he liked to have it. Then he called for me. I did not answer. His steps echoed in the hallway.

I know you're up there, he said.

When I went downstairs, he was in the living room, his back to the fire, his legs spread like an important man.

Show me, he said.

I looked at the floor.

He sighed, Show me what you took from them.

I picked a spot on the carpet to stare at where my dad burned a hole with his cigarette once when he fell asleep.

I said show me the thing you accepted. Now I won't ask you again. I'll tell your father if you don't speak up.

I stared deeper at the burn hole. I imagined shoving Tommy into it. He held out his hand. I took the sweet from my pocket.

He held it between my eyes so close I had to cross them to see it.

This is how it starts, he said.

Remember this, he said and closed his fist around it, and my breath filled with the tears I would not cry for him. He threw it into the fire.

Never do that again, he said. If your father found out.

I didn't do anything.

Tommy shook his head and smiled. I saw you with him, do you think I didn't see you? They don't live in their own country. Can you trust people like that?

I wanted him to stop, so I said, No.

They'll get you to talk to them, to like them.

I won't.

You will.

I won't.

He breathed in and said, I won't, *Tommy*. Please have the courtesy to say my name when you address me.

When I turned to go he said, Whether I tell your father depends on your future behavior. Now go to the supermarket and tell them to go back to their own country. You can say it from the street, and they don't have to hear you.

I don't want to.

I said do it.

I thought of the birds at that moment and what I'd done to them, left them without anything when they sang for me.

Why don't you go back to your own house, I said.

His face darkened like rain. Well, don't you ever—

You're here because you don't have any friends, I said.

Get out, he said. Get out of this room!

After spending the evening in the kitchen to stay out of Tommy's way, I went upstairs and opened the window, saw the stars above the bay so far away, thought that if I ran to them I might meet my mother by accident on the way. I looked at a sailing ship with its string of lights against the mountains and wondered where it was sailing to. I wanted to be on it now, to go where no one would want to talk to me. I called out into the dark for the birds to come back and left them a note pinned under a stone with a drawing on it in pencil of bread and them eating it, so they'd understand what I wanted to say to them, even arrows so they could follow the order. When I was sure they'd be able to see it clearly from the sky I crept into bed, making no noise because Tommy never played the television or the radio. He wore silence on him when he was alone.

I had forgotten to close the window and a breeze blew in—the curtains sailed up and spread and the drawing blew away, a white sheet in the wind. Earlier in the year, when my father and mother had shouted at each other in the night, I did not cry. When my mother left, I had not cried. But I cried now when I heard the paper rustle against the glass and soar off. The birds had nothing to read, and they could not know how much I wanted them to come back.

My father stayed out late. When he came back it was dark and I was still crying. I heard him talk with Tommy and then the bottles opening. Then slow, measured steps counted up the staircase to me, the same way he played the guitar. He entered quietly and sat on the bed. I smelled the drink. He leaned over and switched on the lamp. I kept my eyes closed because they burned from the crying and I was ashamed. I was a big girl and tears were for small girls.

Hello, he said.

I opened my eyes. He looked at me closely and angled the lamp.

You've been crying, he said.

I nodded into the pillow.

Why?

I didn't want to talk about the birds and how they flew away because of what I did. He stroked my hair. You can tell me.

Tommy took up too much space in my mind, so I said about the boy and the sweet instead, and my father didn't seem to mind, nodded at the floor, even when I told him I had gone back to the supermarket with my own sweets.

You traded, he said.

Then I told him about Tommy downstairs throwing it into the fire. My father sat there and didn't move. When I was finished, he waited an extra minute. Then he walked out of the room and down the stairs much faster than he came up. I heard him shout, Get out, and the door slammed. He called from downstairs:

If that man ever even looks at you, you run and find me.

Yes, I said.

He said for me to stay in bed for a while, that he had to get something. I lay waiting until he opened my door half an hour later with two bags of chips and lemonades, and he carried me downstairs where we ate them together in front of the fire. It was almost two o'clock in the morning but I was happier than I'd been in a long time. With Tommy gone, now the world could change. I told my father about the birds and he said we could draw something for them. I ran to my room and brought down a sheet of paper and two pencils, and we drew a picture together: I did the man and he did the woman, the fine brown and black feathers, the tiny beaks and throats, the long spindly legs, a big balloon for writing what they sang, and under them the crumbs and the cap of water.

They'll come back, he said. They will. He put his big hand around me and lay his head in his other hand, and I hid my face in his long hair. Later, he carried me back to bed and stuck the drawing to the window with the picture facing out. I watched him look at the silver line of the mountains under the moon. I would wait with him.

As the weeks passed into months, my mother called more and more, sometimes twice in one day, and my father played guitar without any stops, all the music she would need when she returned. He laughed more than he used to, and my mother sounded happier too. I stayed with people who lived near us, and I ran home every day after playing with my friends, hoping it was the day she came back to us because they were both happy enough again to live together. One day he told me she might be back soon to visit and maybe she might have someone else with her to help them talk, maybe not. I said as long as she came back, I didn't mind if she brought a friend.

That summer when I was ten years old there was much to wish for, even though the months did pass and I never found her when I got home. But I never gave up hope, and in the late afternoons when the long days stretched before me, I convinced myself that I could already hear singing in all the windows, upstairs and downstairs. I waved goodbye to the kind people who looked after me and hopped along the street, running in the sunlight, dancing in the sunlight, taking the shortest way back to the vast countryside of my father's empty house, the house where we once lived with birds.

THE RECEPTIONIST

MY WIFE WAS DRIVEN OFF in a black car this afternoon by a man who steered along the drive down to the street and turned right out the gate. I saw her gloved fingers flick a cigarette through the slit in the window. The city skyline turned from morning white to mid-morning sea blue, and now my wife was still somewhere under that sky. I had hoped she would return by lunch, but lunch came and went, and when five o'clock struck, I thought I might go to the bedroom to check. It was likely full of her shoes, her dresses, her perfume. She was mistaken if she thought I was going to stand around an empty house and wait for her. I was going downtown myself, as simple as that. Before leaving, I walked the slope of the garden under the shade of the willow and checked the kitchen windows. The rose thorns under them bent and crunched underfoot. One of them scraped my thigh. The windows were locked. The bedroom curtains were open a crack, the linen so fresh I could smell it even from the garden. Sunlight was every-where, its hands playing the rooms like white keys.

The Receptionist

I drove down the winding tree-lined street we lived on
and registered at a hotel in the town. The receptionist didn't
look at me once during registration. He managed to hand
me the key and direct me to the room, all the while looking
at a button on my shirt. I paused after thanking him, and I
told him again this thing was temporary, but the man turned
and put his feet up in front of the portable television under
the desk counter. The carpets were dirty, the hallways dark.
The number on the door was chipped, so I could not tell
exactly if it was mine, but no one screamed when I entered.
The light from the hall let me see the outline of the bed and
the lamp below a brass-framed painting of horses dashing
along the surf. I locked the door behind me and undressed in
the dark: shoes off, belt unbuckled, shirt loosened, drawing
right and left sides evenly away from the chest. Outside, the
cobblestone courtyard extended to the street, the breeze
pleasant in my hair, the party on High Street all the way to
the Spanish Arch. At least at a hotel I had company, even if
the atmosphere was suitcases and the usual urgency, people
new to town and looking for a cheap place to stay and the
good time they knew must be found somewhere. Tomorrow
I would have breakfast before going back to the house and
greeting my wife. She might want to know where I had been.
I would not ask her where she'd been. But now I lay on the
covers with palms open at my sides and listened to the music
from the street below.

My heart beat faster. Such an instrument, the heart: it
senses emotion and plays it back instantly in the only language it knows, those beats along the arteries like a child
with its tiny, hopeful, attentive hands. I placed mine on the
center of my chest and waited for the flutter. I waited for

the anger, but I saw my wife's tongue on her lover's lips in the dark. I saw him moving his hand across her cheek. If I really loved her I would feel more emotion for her than I did for a rude and sullen hotel desk clerk, a complete stranger who maddened me just now with his indifference. I turned to one side and drew my knees up. When I shut my eyes tightly, the yellows and reds circled. Where did those lights come from? Where did they go?

In the next room a woman said something, a man said something. I jumped from the bed and ran to the wall and put my ear there. Could have been her voice. I must do something but not go down to that receptionist and give him the satisfaction of watching my shirt button as he sits grinning and shaking his head, saying that this is a hotel. Someone walked around, opening and shutting drawers. I dressed and paced, and then I imagined throwing myself against the door and wrestling him to the ground while shouting at the top of my voice for help. What kind of help, that might occur to me at some point. The man with my wife was breaking no law. So the plan dissolved. And what if a strange couple was draped arm in arm when I crashed through the door? I looked out the window, down to the courtyard.

It was dark, I must have slept a few hours after I checked in. A two-foot ledge ran along the outer ivy-covered wall. I stepped out. My shirt rode up to my neck and the ivy scraped my skin. I stood on the small balcony and leaned over the edge for the window next door, but the curtains were drawn. A woman called briefly from the dark behind me in the courtyard. I swayed, clutching the iron rails. In the alley thirty feet below, one shadow bent over another under the streetlight's glare, the woman's dress around her hips. They passed the streetlight, embracing tightly, voices muffled until she laughed and he grabbed her waist. They were swaying back into the light, a pair out for the night, singing now, singing their way to the grass by the river.

In the morning I woke to more noise in the courtyard, the sun warm on the bed. I walked to the window and saw a crowd chatting at the breakfast tables. Toast, coffee, waitresses flitting among the tables, trays of glasses, knives and forks, red linen cloth. I went down and took a chair facing the hotel windows, ordered a glass of orange juice and toast, and opened the newspaper. Sunday morning in Galway. I would shortly be going home to my wife, steering up the drive to the front porch and revving the engine so that she could hear me, and then to the living room. Some sort of passion would save us.

After breakfast I walked to the desk and asked the receptionist, slouched over in a doze, for the name of the person or people in the room next to mine.

I can't tell you that, he said. I can't tell you who is in the next room, or in any of the other rooms. This you know already. The English was foreign English, those words weren't the ones he grew up talking.

I want to stay another night, I said.

I'm not going to stop you.

He pushed the registration book an inch in my direction. I scratched my name and paid the man.

I have great courage in the morning. I should have done this last night. I marched to the room next door, knocked and stood back. If my wife answered, at least she was alive and well. No further questions. Division of property. Handshake.

Shuffling. I knocked again, louder.

Answer the door, I said. This is the receptionist.

The door opened to a single, cold eye and a man's voice. Well?

Is everything all right? I said.

You are not the receptionist.

He shut the door before I saw anything. I put my ear to it in case she was in there. Downstairs I slapped a note in front of the man at the desk and asked for change. He did not take his eye off the television as he opened the till, put my note in, and placed five euro on the counter.

Five euro? I said.

Five in every five-euro note. No more, no less.

I gave you a ten.

He turned in his seat and smiled at my stomach with two bad teeth riddled with plaque. He laughed and scratched the hair under his white cap, pulled the till entirely out of its drawer and placed it on the table. A single note lay by the silver and brass piles.

You gave me this. No more, no less.

Is there a phone in the hotel?

He motioned with his thumb. I called our number at home, waited for my wife or the answering machine. After ten rings I hung up.

The receptionist ignored me when I got back to the desk.

Any messages? I said.

Since when? He turned the page of a magazine.

Since I was here a few minutes ago.

No.

My key, please.

He slammed it on the counter.

I walked the threadbare red carpet to the stairs. At the top, the corridor and a single bulb a spider drew to the wall with its web. I turned the key in the lock of my room, undressed carefully and placed my clothes at the end of the bed and stretched out on the covers.

The curtains waved a breeze into the room, an image into my head. I am standing at the top of the hotel staircase. My wife appears at the bottom of the stairs. She is wearing a scarf that flows behind her as she runs towards me, frightened, though we have never argued, never fought. We withered. She knows I visit the house when she is away. She has written through her solicitor. But I see even in the legal writing that there is enough love left for one of us. She reaches my embrace and looks back. The receptionist is almost upon her. His head is raised, his eyes swill down to a focus, but he is looking at me, not her. He does not understand. He wants to end my pain.

NEW DEAL

THE IMMIGRANT IN HIS NEW uniform blubbered away his English and left me with a dribble I couldn't understand. What are you saying to me, I said, but he was lost to me now. It was numbers I wanted from him, not words.

He gaped at his stomach as if it might go away, the bullet in it, if he looked hard enough.

I have to learn to talk to you, is that it? I said.

Hatty came around the van and waved at me: Let him be, we have the bags, he said, dragging the first one to the open door of the car.

I stepped over the new uniform bleeding on the ground and asked him if he wanted me to finish it. Somehow he understood or didn't and shook his head. So I let him be, this man, even did him a favor: the shot was a small caliber and nothing to keep him long from a wife and family. He goes back to the job three months later a hero because he challenged us, put his life in danger for a firm that paid him a pittance to guard a small fortune, and I gave him that choice. You won't hear that in the news. We burned the car and spent the night in a ditch.

We were by one of those side roads to the border, huddled inside our coats and speaking of old times, the way both sides killed each other then. Because the rain filled it like any other, we didn't even know if it was the right ditch, but it was night and we had to hide somewhere.

The birds woke before sunrise, cold and tight in their nests. I moved my feet and felt the mud shift between my toes. I watched Hatty rest lightly, as if he were outside sleep and waiting for it with his eyes closed. He was called that name because he took to wearing caps when he lost some hair on the crown. It was a sore point evidently. If sleep had indeed come for him, it did him no good with the dream it threw his way: he woke and said he saw in the headlights of his dream a baby born in a hospital, and as the nurses delivered the healthy boy, they noticed he did not cry as most infants do, and in the child's hands they found this tiny plastic gray knife. When they tried to take it from him the baby cried, and so they had to remove it over some hours by cutting it with a real blade. The child was inconsolable. Hatty said all this in the manner of someone still waking up, when a man is more likely to speak the truth.

That is a strange dream, I said.

The first delivery trucks went by, swishing more water over us. Hatty nodded off again with the pistol on his lap, his chin buried in his elbow, until I tapped him on the shoulder.

He's here.

A large truck stopped gently over fifty yards and we sat into the small cab space behind the driver. We crossed the border into the flat countryside and then along the coast north. The blue sea appeared to the right hugged the vision in and out of the hills. I changed into a pullover as the heater blasted warm dust into my face. The trucker stopped for tea in a village and stuck his face in a newspaper in the café, so we walked outside to get some air, the way a couple of ordinary fellows would. The truck was carrying sheep packed into the long trailer eight or ten abreast: here and there along the sides a hoof stuck out through the air vents, wriggling as an animal tried to bring it back inside. I walked up to the side of the trailer and peered in: all dark, stuck here and there with white. The stench moved me back, the shapes and shuffling and scraping around a larger silence. Hatty, cursing about cruelty, unlatched the backboard and swung the doors open. Sheep tumbled out like foam, tottering and jostling as they found balance. They milled around the truck until he scattered them into the surrounding fields. When we looked back, the trucker was coming at us with a length of pipe. It was funny to watch him and Hatty was going to shoot him, but I reminded him that he was on the wrong side of the border for that, and in the end we ran among the sheep that raced in fitful bursts, scattering out in circles on the soft bog ground. The partial shouts ground against the chill of the air:

I'll fucking. I'll get.

After a few hard yards of running, the trucker gave up. The sheep were all over the place. One of them was trapped on a barbed-wire fence. It struggled and I tore the hooks from the wool or whatever Hatty said was a sheep's hide. I helped the sheep because the trucker swore at me, and I'd be seeing him again in any case.

We didn't worry about the bags because we'd left them back in the ditch. They were picked up by someone else who drove them across the border and left them in a blue car. We picked up the blue car from the car park where the sheep truck stopped. The bags were tight in the back. It was a short drive to the ferry across the fields. The weather was pleasant, fresh on the skin. Clouds jostled the blue into smaller and smaller spaces. I could smell the salt. At noon we took a dirt track and walked up the winding incline to the rocks and seaweed. A mile offshore, the island appeared to sit at most an inch or two above the waves, an occasional refuge for me with two pubs and the constabulary that comes to visit only when there's trouble. We sat on a pier bench and waited. The coarse sea grass leaned in the wind. The blue harbor water formed tiny crests under the dot of the ferry, which we watched until the engine tapped to us like Morse across the water.

Never on time, that man. The white hair of Coyne the ferryman blew about his forehead as he scanned the empty docking area without ever looking directly at us. Not many ferrymen look relieved when they see only a couple of people waiting. The wind whistled around the rope as he flung it to us. Five minutes into the crossing, with the blue car roped to the railings, Coyne switched the radio on in the ferry wheelhouse, took the whistling kettle off the burner and poured three cups before tapping on the wheelhouse window. Hatty went in and slammed the door against the bluster and the rocking. I leaned on the car and watched the two of them.

For thirty years now there had indeed been a war between two slogans, our day will come and never give up an inch. Then it was all nice between everyone and we adapted to the business after war. For thirty years we defended housing estates and parts of streets, and now it was the time to do something with them. When you have an army you don't disband and let common criminals come in. Some did test the waters, a few lads from London trying to blend in and sell some pills. Some left quickly, some didn't.

We had to trust someone. Naturally we thought of each other. When you have to trust people, make sure to trust people you hate. This was a test delivery across the border from the south to the north to figure out together the safe roads and houses that we'd already figured out separately. They sent us Hatty, an old timer: word was he had taken care of a number of our side. Now that's trust for you, to send us someone like him, and for him to agree. Once the money was counted he'd wander off home across the border and we'd put it to work.

The handing over of the tea in the wheelhouse seemed to be taking a sentence or two longer than it should have. Coyne saw me looking and pushed open the wheelhouse door and negotiated the distance over to me in a flapping cape, puffing at his pipe.

He moved at my shoulder. Are you here for a few days?

I am here minding my own business.

Good enough. He blew some smoke. Only asking.

Coyne was always only asking, always giving me some kind of an eye. The cape flapped off his body and filled the view.

What, Hatty mouthed at the glass when I signaled him.

Will you help me unload the car? I said after he joined us.

Hatty held on to his cap. All you have to do is drive it off the ferry.

Coyne shouted into the wind, What? He raised his arm and pointed to the island out of the spray that hit the deck.

I'm just asking this man to help me get the car off, I said.

But Coyne was in the wheelhouse again and bringing us parallel to a shingle beach. I knew this wasn't the regular docking place, not the dock at the scattered fishing boats that lined the small raised harbor wall. I ran after him.

What fucking place is this?

Coyne's cape rose up behind his head as he spoke. I'm not landing this car at the regular spot.

But on a beach?

The sand is a stone mix. It's my ferry and I land where I want to. I'll drive it off for you.

He dropped anchor and tied off against a bollard and sat behind the car wheel when I gave him the key. Hatty ran down to the gritty sand, lowered the ramp and gave the signal. Coyne released the parking brake and the car rolled down. It sank up to the chrome in the mud between the end of the ramp and the yellow sand, a matter of two feet more and he'd have been fine. He turned in his seat and looked behind him as if ready to back up and try again.

I said, You thick, fucking bastard.

We put sticks under it and Coyne and Hatty pushed at the car for ten minutes. The fast tide ebbed and the ferry would soon settle. Coyne got into the wheelhouse and gunned the ferry engine until the ramp nudged the back of the rear tires; I got behind the wheel of the Ford, my hot breath staining the small glass as I wound down the side window, stuck my face out into the biting salt air and put the car into reverse, moved it back up the ramp. They put more sticks down and then I let the car slide, engaging second gear at the last moment. The bumper grazed the sand and the wheels bounced the car up and away. I kept driving, said thick bastards again into the rearview mirror at the two of them talking again as if they knew each other all the time. Hatty was on the wrong side of the border for that kind of forgiveness, and it wasn't his to give.

The town was a minute's drive along the twisting road. I drove to the island butcher shop. The place smelled of carcasses and sawdust on a concrete floor. The butcher appeared, wiping his hands in the apron blood.

What are we having today, then? he said.

Do you have a turkey? I said.

The butcher righted his spectacles. One turkey.

He came out of the cold room holding a puckered bag of skin by the legs and slapped it onto the counter while flashing the knife. He cut the string and pushed his arm into the aperture between the legs, creating a sucking sound. Music poked from the cassette player that dangled from a ceiling meat hook, a waltz, and it filtered along the white wall.

That's Mozart, the butcher said as he pulled out a string of insides that came loose with dull thuds of suction. They were entwined in pale colors like cooked spaghetti, dotted with nodules of dripping fat. He dunked them into a tin pail and scoured along the inner skin with a large spoon, extracted the insides carefully and walked on tiptoe to the pail, trying not to spill the viscous lining. I swallowed at the stench of gas and took a step back. The butcher repeated this, inserting his glove-red arm until only an odd lump or two remained on the spoon after a scouring, then felt around inside for more. When the turkey was clean, the butcher wrapped it and nodded goodbye before taking the pail out the rear exit, whistling to his dog. I took the skewered turkey wrapped in foil and walked quickly to the car. I left the bags in the cold room where the turkey came from.

I then went to the address Hatty had been given to wait. I was outside the window of the house when it happened: I was holding a gun and those two bullets pushed Hatty right back headfirst into the mirror, those two bullets took a good part of that man's skull and finished the business quickly. Do it before a man gets to thinking too much about what he's facing, send him there and he'll figure it out just as well. They'd send a younger lad next, someone with less history about him. We used to kill for country, now we had something we could count. I followed the road farther along the coast until it went up the cliff face, became a lane and then dirt. I faced the blue Ford out to sea with its headlights into the twilight. Then I walked down the cliff slope and to the harbor café and sipped at a cup of tea where a window faced the cliff.

Coyne soon came in and swept the room with the same eyes he swept the dock on the mainland, saw me and didn't see me. He sat at the counter and ordered apple pie with the yogurt instead of ice cream, everything cold, being nice to the young one on her summer holidays from someplace with her hair tied up and smiling all the time. I often found him here or in the pub next door, the two busiest places along the harbor wall. On the odd weekend I stayed on the island I'd walk the ten minutes to the bright café along the single, dark street filled with talk and the smell of fish. And every night he came for no reason other than to sit there at that counter and drink coffee and chat with whomever sat nearby. He must have often felt he had the time to be able to sit in the soft lights of the café in full view of everyone's business and hear conversation everywhere around him in the late hour until he felt sleepy enough to go home. I suppose he was only fending off the silence. But he never talked to me, and often we were the only two at the counter in the very late hours. My affliction was boredom, yet I went out into company to stay alone, and that meant not talking to Coyne. The smiling young girl from someplace learned to move between us and talk to one at a time.

His daughter, Mary, walked in the door and approached him.

Where were you, Daddy?

I had to wait on the other side a little longer, that's all.

You said you wouldn't work the ferry today. I said I'd do it for you.

He stood and drank some milk, swilled it around in his mouth. His daughter moved a hand through his white beard and hugged him. I looked away. The car was still at the cliff edge, the headlights still strong.

I went next door to the pub. It was ten o'clock, and Hatty hadn't arrived. Some men in the back room played games on a table and one of them walked past me and ordered a round of pints and chasers, some peanuts. The owner wiped the counter even though it was clean. The back-room door opened, and I heard, Where is that Fenian fuck, and after a minute some shouts. On the television in the corner was the night news, the details of a robbery. At half past ten the committee rolled out of the pub. I bent to my drink, watching them leave in a slow line with their drinks and some bottles, the door swinging open and shut along the chain. One pointed to the cliffs, something about the lights. They peeled away in bent twos. I saw them file up to the headlights. A half an hour later they had not come down, so I followed by another route, coming silently to a rise behind the car. The men were invisible but they were here. I watched the lights of the café, still bright, behind the harbor wall. The pub was dark.

A shape came up the slope to the cliff edge, stopping possibly to check if he was being followed or to enjoy the view of the town below with the faintly illuminated threads of light leaning south in the night wind. Now he was near enough and checked behind him again. He approached the car and must have seen the sheet on the seat covering a man.

Two of them unwrapped the dark off them and pinned him from behind.

Coming up to check on your work, is that it?

They bundled him into the back seat and left the doors wide open on both sides and crowded them. Two of the men lifted the sheet. Hatty's face was upturned, the eyes open, his skin torn. Two holes in his face glistened in the interior bulb. They covered him again. Coyne tried to turn away but they held him fixed. One of the others lit up a cigarette and blew it at him.

I didn't kill him, Coyne said. He looked into the dark for me, must have felt I was there, the way a man uses some new sense when he's about to lose them all.

So who then?

It wasn't me.

At some point Coyne must have thought of Mary and smelled the lavender and saffron from her hair, what I smelled when she came into the café earlier, where she said she had prepared a sweet dish for when he got home that evening. Now the ferryman had to breathe the smoke that sailed along the dashboard, felt the wind buffet the car and whisk it off. They began to hit him. He sank deeper into the small vinyl seat. His ears and mouth flamed up like a struck match, I could see the damage from where I lay. He moved to free the cramp invading his legs, but there was no room. He rattled at the door handle, but it was closed now. The car must have seemed to shrink around him and the windshield dissolve as shovels of rain smeared across the glass and buried him in the ground of the weather. They struck him with sticks. They ripped him with glass. Coyne slapped the side window and screamed once. The men outside opened the door and dragged him from the car. He fell onto the grass. They stood in a circle and kicked.

Coyne clutched at the grass. He must have heard the water against the rocks eighty feet down. They lifted him to his feet.

Don't take me from my daughter. I didn't kill anyone. I'm seventy years old.

They shoved him into a run toward the cliff edge, where he grabbed at a seagull in the headlights and fell grabbing through it. The committee waited, but it was too windy for the splash, or else the tide was out, that was another question.

They crowded in around the dead Hatty and drank a toast from the bottles. They turned the radio on and watched the weak projection of the headlights capture the brief outline of birds as they flew by. Sometimes one soared across the bright, sometimes two. The leader pulled the sheet off Hatty once more. His mouth was open and his face wet. Flies peppered the vinyl roof. At two a.m. the lights were long gone and the radio out, so they sang until the last one fell asleep. In the dead of night a sea bird screeched and one of the men, I don't know who, screamed awake, swinging a punch.

HARRY DIETZ

MR. DIETZ'S EYES SNAPPED open and he gasped, clutched the sheets on his bed and squeezed them until he knew where he was, until familiar shapes emerged like ghosts from the dark to reassure him: the Venetian blinds slicing the streetlight across his robe folded on the chair, his ties draped on a coat hanger, his radio with the red 5:34 that burned like embers on his bedside table. He let his breath straighten out in a sigh. Another long nightmare in a short night.

Mr. Dietz fixed his glasses, switched on the bedside light, and shut the alarm off, even though it was set for 7:30, because he often forgot to turn it off when he woke this early and it wasn't one of those new ones that shut itself off. Occasionally when he came back in the evening from work he'd hear the thing ringing even from the parking lot and find an angry letter in the slit of his mailbox from his downstairs neighbours, Mr. and Mrs. Shaw. After reading the angry letter he'd go to their door. Apologies, promises to buy a newer model, one that shut itself off after a few minutes. Afterward he would go upstairs, and by the time he had switched on his television, Mr. Shaw and his wife and their complaints had faded.

Once upon a time, whenever that was—and he often wondered when once upon a time was—Dietz's moods started to come and go like pages of a book flapping in a breeze until everything he knew lay scattered like fallen playing cards; but then his brain sometimes flashed, even burst into happy flames, and he felt better and saw better each moment of his life, it seemed, back to his first steps as a child.

About ten years ago he had gone to the town doctor, a man with teeth bulging out of a smile under gold-rimmed glasses, and told the fellow that he was waking too early every morning and that he felt down about things. The doctor slapped Harry on the back and told him to keep his chin up, that things would turn around, to think of all the fine people in his life, that everyone got the blues at some point in their lives. Then the doctor guided him out of the office. Weeks later Dietz went back and this time the doctor gave him some pills, but they made him fall asleep at work, sprawled over his calculator, so he stopped taking them, at least in the morning. He kept them in the fridge.

But this time of the morning was his, and Dietz imagined that Mr. Shaw and his wife were still asleep, a few feet under his bedroom floorboards in their long, straight bed.

Five thirty-eight in the morning. Dietz knotted his robe at the front and walked along the dark corridor to the kitchen. When the fridge door opened, a bulb lit his face, and he remembered that he'd only gone to bed a few hours before because of that late-night film and because he had to play with the coat hanger to get a good picture on the television.

Let's see. No milk. No coffee without milk.

Best go to Fred's.

Mr. Dietz pressed his feet into his moccasin loafers, pulled his gray jacket over the red bathrobe to offset the chill of a late April dawn and strode out to his Ford Zephyr. As the Ford bounced onto the street, Dietz went over in his mind how to get to Fred's place, and he pulled up to the store in three minutes.

Hi, Fred.

Fred looked up from the floor in front of the drinks cooler where he was unpacking a box and waved.

Hi, Harry. Up early again I see.

Dietz fished for coins. Yep. Thought I'd get a head start on those figures for the inventory on Monday.

Coffee, Harry?

Yes, and milk, please.

Leave it on the counter, Harry. I'll see you tomorrow.

I've just got a twenty.

Take the change out of the till, bang on it, it'll open.

How much? said Dietz.

Take sixteen dollars and eighty-five cents.

Okay, I'm taking sixteen dollars and eighty-five cents.

That's fine, Harry.

Harry poured some coffee and put his milk in a brown bag. He stood by his car and sipped, looked up once at the first infusion of milk into the night sky. It was as fine and crisp a Saturday morning as he'd seen in a while.

While driving back to his apartment, Harry turned into a small street on an impulse because his headlights caught a street sign that rang a bell, but he couldn't say why until he cruised the row of houses. The shapes suggested images that cleared away the confusion like condensation you rub off a window with your sleeve. The street, he knew, had pulled him to it because it had something for him. Her name was Mary Norman.

She once worked with him at Beodeker's Electronics in Charleston, Illinois, after they left high school—they were twenty-one and in love; it was 1962, and after five years of dating, they cruised this street one day and selected the home they'd live in if they were married, and then Dietz had asked her if she'd marry him—not that he was ready to ask, but his dad once told Harry he thought too much and should be more assertive with people. So he took a deep breath and asked Mary across in the passenger seat, 'Will you marry me?' But he didn't actually ask her until a few minutes later, when he spoke the words out loud.

Now Harry slowed down as he passed the house with the double chimney, the one he and Mary selected so long ago before he popped the question in the front seat while he sipped on a soda, staring straight ahead. Mary had smiled, looked straight ahead too, said she'd think about it. But the weeks turned into months and Mary never said yes. She put it off, never explaining why, until one day she told him nervously in his office at the store that she had found someone else, another friend, someone who made her laugh, and that she was sorry to let Harry down like that, but that laughing was important in a man.

He never found anyone else. Not after that. Mary Norman, it turns out, was dating and eventually married the store owner, Mr. Beodeker. Harry had thought about speaking to Mr. Beodeker, but he couldn't figure out how to bring up the subject. So many ways to say the same thing: Mr. Beodeker, this customer wants to know why his record keeps skipping, and after you've handled that, I'd like to know why you stole my girlfriend.

Harry kept her photo in his wallet clipped to his driver's license. He turned onto another street. He had lived in Charleston all his life, but most of the streets were not familiar to him. He figured that the next turn would bring him back to Fred's, and from there he could get home again and have his coffee. That street, however, did not bring him back to Fred's; instead he found himself driving on bigger and longer roads, and soon he had to shield his face against the rising sun, so he changed direction, moved down a ramp onto a highway, and the sun swung to the right and the road opened wide like a grey flower in front of him.

He was heading north.

The highway sign read Chicago 195 miles. He liked the idea. *Chicago?* Why the hell not, why not! It was as good as lounging around the apartment. He tasted his coffee and felt a lift but quickly braked it down to fifty-five. The car behind him swerved. He hadn't driven on a highway for the longest time, hated it—too many people speeding and tailgating—but today the paved road invited him like a warm canal. He pressed to his head the hat he kept in the glove compartment, wrapped his hands over the steering wheel and pursed his lips, glad that he'd decided to do it, and it was the weekend, the right time to travel. As he drove through the flat fields of southern Illinois he rolled down the window and smelled the fertilizer. Bits of the landscape rolled across the windshield: gas station signs on towers, exit ramps to small towns off the interstate, a pickup that was broken down on the shoulder with the hood raised and a red rag knotted on the antenna. It felt good to be on a trip, much better than he felt earlier. Why did he have to drive to feel better? His dressing gown blew about his face so much he stuffed it down under the seatbelt, and despite the jacket, he wondered now why he didn't go back to dress in regular clothes for the trip.

Cars passed. He saw drivers shaving, combing hair, applying makeup in the rear-view mirror. One driver read a book. A few miles down the highway Harry slammed on the brakes and stopped in the slow lane. The line of cars behind him squeezed into a tight squeal of brakes and fought each other for lane space fifty yards back. Faces shouted at him as they passed his driver's side window. He put a finger to his lips and frowned; he had stopped because he remembered that when he was pouring the coffee at Fred's he'd glanced at the morning newspapers wrapped in a bundle on the floor. On the header he reread in his mind the words 'Friday, April 24, 1999'.

Friday! Harry drove off to the shoulder and sped up again to fifty-five, mortified that he was driving to Chicago on a work day. Friday! Mr. Beodeker would not be amused. Seven miles later he pulled off the road, drove up to a gas station and called the store while the attendant filled his tank.

Hello? This is Mr. Dietz. Is Mr. Beodeker there? He's busy? Can I leave a message? Tell him I'll not be in today. No, I'm not sick—yes, I'll call later.

He shook his head as he replaced the receiver. Someone spoke behind him:

You going my way?

He turned to the voice. A thin boy of about twenty, looking at Dietz's bathrobe.

I'm just out for some coffee and milk, Dietz said.

I'd really appreciate some help, the boy said. He stood at the window of the diner beside the station. In fact, I'm kind of hungry.

Harry studied the boy's face because he looked familiar. Did you work at the store a few years back?

The boy swallowed. What?

Beodeker's in Charleston. I think I remember you.

The boy steadied himself. Yeah, I worked there for a couple of weeks. I got fired. You've got one hell of a memory.

Dietz said, I owe the station ten bucks, but I'll put it on my credit card; that leaves me some cash. Let's get something to eat.

I'm John, said the boy, and shook Dietz's hand.

Mr. Dietz, Harry said.

They sat in the diner. The boy talked about his plans as he ate. Upwardly mobile after a tough year. Sick and tired of Charleston. An investment idea involving old cell phones. Dietz nodded occasionally, dipping his eyes to take a bite out of his burger.

You still working for old Beodeker? John said.

Yep. Still there, never left, never will.

Earn enough?

Enough to live on, for what I need.

I'll bet the old bastard is still paying you six bucks an hour.

Eight. I went up to eight four years ago. I'm on the top scale for the position.

John had bright eyes, and Harry remembered them: they

made the young boy very appealing. John had worked in his department but was different from the other college boys that the store hired part-time, most of whom laughed at the idiot Dietz when he asked them questions about how the new electronic gadgets worked. Life had been fine in the late fifties and sixties when he could take apart a Zenith or a Hotpoint and make a day's work out of them, but now the store was full of MP3 players, notebook computers, and God knows what coming out next, and he spent most of the day in the office, tapping his calculator, refilling his coffee cup. When customers asked about a new product, he'd call one of the boys over and excuse himself. Harry often wondered why Mr. Beodeker hadn't fired him.

But dependable John had helped, always coming into the office and patiently telling him what to say to the customer, even writing responses for him on a slip that Harry could read from the counter as he answered the customer. Harry was sorry when John got fired.

Opposite him, John's mouth was moving, and the words assembled in Harry's brain.

What do you call a boomerang that doesn't come back? John said.

I don't know. A boomerang that doesn't work?

No, John said. A stick.

For the first time in twenty years Harry laughed from his belly. The steel clock on the diner wall read 11:04, and John sat back, patting his stomach.

Thanks, Mr. Dietz. You were always a decent guy.

Harry hadn't finished, so John ordered some apple pie. Harry watched him a moment and said, You know, I never knew your second name.

Donnolly, John Donnolly. My parents moved here and then I was born.

And that's an Irish name, Harry said. My mother was Irish.

And your father?

German. So we're both Irish then, Harry said.

We're Irish, John said.

Harry held the hamburger loosely in both sets of fingertips: Two Irishmen. Fancy that now.

John stabbed the apple pie. You ever been there?

Harry lifted the hamburger an inch closer to his mouth, My father said we should go back to Ireland, he met my mother there when he was a student, and he said I should see where she came from. My mother wanted to go. But the scare put a stop to that.

The scare?

Harry glanced at the ceiling and down: The bomb. The Russians.

The boy shook his head. Where is there safer than Ireland? The castles, right? As green as fuck, dancing at the crossroads. The nukes would fly overhead.

Is that what your parents told you? Harry said.

All the time. What do you know? You weren't even there.

That's true, Harry said. But my mother said there was a reason she left. I never knew what it was, but she wasn't in a hurry to go back for a long time, and then she started telling my father that things must have changed, that maybe they could visit. So something has changed in that country.

I'm going to go one day, John said. I should see it at least once.

That you should, Harry said. We both should.

John pointed his fork with apple dangling: Why don't you go over?

Harry spoke in the space around the hamburger, They wouldn't have an old man, not in a million years.

John swallowed the last of the pie and looked at the empty plate. Yeah, but you can fix radios. I remember you doing that shit with those things people brought in. They must have old radios in Ireland. You could get a job.

They'd turn me back at the bridge. I have to go to the bathroom, John.

In the bathroom Harry retied the belt on his gown and washed his hands in front of the mirror. John was a nice boy, though he got fired from the store, a mistake of some kind over money or something, and he was gone one day. Harry thought he might ask John if he wanted to go to Ireland. If he did, Harry would ask the boy's father and mother if they minded. They could go next week, get a fast passport and go. Lately he had run out of life, the emptiness was pouring into his head. Harry moved a hand across his shaven head. A woman once told him he had big, kind eyes. He did not see them now. He saw an old man's eyes and what they did not see.

Even from the other side of the diner he saw that John was gone. But they hadn't passed each other. Harry sat down and waited for him to come back. The waitress sauntered over with the bill on a cracked saucer. She eyed his gown and moccasins.

Are you lost, sir?

No, I don't believe so. I'm just out for some coffee and milk, that's all.

He decided to check the restroom again, but it was empty. He called John's name in the hope that he was in one of the cubicles, but some man shouted angrily, No, leave me alone, and so Harry went to the front of the diner and pressed his face to the glass and scanned the parking area. No sign.

He turned to the stares of customers and reached for his wallet to pay the bill, but he'd left it in his jacket, and the jacket was gone. Harry walked back to the restroom to look for it since he'd just been there. Nothing. He looked under the cubicles and the angry man flung open the cubicle door and pushed him, asked him what his problem was. Then Harry went back to the front of the diner and stared out the window and watched his Ford for a few minutes because it was the only thing he knew.

His father had given a Ford to him around the time he was courting Mary, so Harry bought another Ford when he needed to replace the first, which strangely enough had stopped working the year his dad died. That was the time Harry had an argument with Mary because she had opened the bag in which he kept his father's record collection. This happened a week after he asked her to marry him, when she was still thinking about his proposal. He had caught her sifting though his father's old 78s on his settee one morning and grabbed them from her. With the records in one hand he stalked the room looking for the bag. He shouted his accusation bitterly. She had opened the bag and let the smoke out, the smell of the cigarettes his father had smoked. The bag preserved the smell that was in his father's house the day of the funeral, when Harry had securely packed and sealed the records. He had shouted at

Mary for a long time and she had cried. He wanted to seal them up again but it was too late because the ordinary air had mixed in. She told him never to speak to her like that again.

That's when she took up with Beodeker, he was sure of it.

Sir?

Harry turned from the diner window to the waitress who held the bill out to him.

Would you like to pay this? she said.

Yes, but my wallet is gone. My jacket is gone.

She shrugged, You want me to get the manager, is that what you want?

If you wouldn't mind.

Stay right there.

She went to the rear of the diner and spoke to a young man who wound his way through the tables and looked Harry up and down.

You'll have to pay. You ate the food, the young man said.

Of course I'm going to pay. Harry reached into the pocket of his robe and retrieved sixteen dollars and eighty-five cents. The manager turned to the waitress. The waitress took the money from Dietz's hand.

She said, I didn't mean to be rude just now.

Harry smiled. I'm on an unexpected trip.

She lifted her hand in a goodbye as he left the diner. After another hour on the highway Harry grew tired, as he always did in the early afternoon. He pulled over into a rest area and dozed in the front seat. When he straightened himself up, the sun had moved left of center in the sky, and the shadows of trees in the fields lengthened toward him.

Walking over to a payphone, he fumbled a coin into the payphone slot and dialed the store.

I'm sorry to call this late in the day, Mr. Beodeker, but I wanted to explain—I don't know what happened—

What? I don't know what you mean—of course I still work there—

Harry rushed to the car. For some reason Mr. Beodeker seemed to think that Harry hadn't worked there for a month, that his position had been filled two weeks ago.

Maybe that's why he had driven all this way today. That was it, he'd show Mr. Beodeker. Harry pulled out of the rest area and chugged over to the fast lane without signaling. The highway behind him gyrated with pressed horns, fists out of windows. After another hour the signs for Chicago grew bigger and the traffic seemed to close in around him. People switched on their headlights as the light drained from the west. Harry drove in the fast lane and then slowed back to the speed limit. People flashed their headlights behind him. He turned the AM radio up loud to keep himself alert. A talk show host interviewing a man who had written a book about alien abductions in the Chicago area, and Harry heard the man say on the air, loud as you please, that viruses weren't the only threat facing Americans.

What do you mean when you say that there are other threats facing Americans, the interviewer said. My listeners want to know.

The Russians are what I mean. The Russians, with the help and assistance of our president, are conducting secret training camps in western Montana, crack Russian troops.

What now, you mean the Russians are coming?

No, sir, that's not what I'm telling you. I'm telling you that the Russians are here.

What's the purpose? I mean, what do they hope to achieve?

To strike at the right moment. We're weak now, with the war and everything, fighting on so many fronts. We fight the terror and the reds sneak in.

Frightening, the host said. This is truly monumental. Folks, our number is 800.456.9982. We'll take more phone calls after these messages. Are the Russians coming? Are they already here? Your calls after these messages.

Harry gripped the steering wheel and looked around him. The sky balanced day and evening, and lights swarmed in the rear-view mirror. Cars overtook him filled with shapes hunched over or lying back fleetingly in his vision: soldiers, agents, advance people. His mouth hung open and his eyes widened as he razed the mirror with glances. Russians? He remembered his father calling to him from the doorway. He was nine, and they had bought a fallout shelter. His father hurried him to the bottom of the yard and asked him where to build it. Harry pointed to a bunch of big green nettles. The Communists might drop a big bomb on the town, his father said, but Harry and he would survive in the shelter for months if it happened. His father swung his spade and dug and dug, yelling at Harry to go into the house and bring him water, or to take his handkerchief and wipe his forehead.

The Communists won't wait for us to finish. Look up at the sky, Harry. Look up at the sky while I'm digging. If you see a trail of smoke, it's the atom bomb coming for us.

So Harry watched the sky until his father yelled at him again for something else. He smelled the wood kit boxes and the wet-cement stink when it was finished. The next week was boiling hot, and one morning while Harry stood in the garden with his toy airplane, his father ran out of the house in his long black trousers and jacket and yanked him by the shoulder.

Quick! Quick! The shelter! We've less than a minute!

Harry dropped the plane and tried to look up into the blue but he lost his footing as his father dragged him along. Harry said, But Lucky. I want Lucky to come too.

Lucky can't come. The dog will foul the air. We have to seal it tight. Get in there, Harry.

And his father pushed him in and closed the door between them, the door with the three yellow triangles, and all of a sudden it was pitch black and Harry's breath bounced in his chest so hard it hurt.

Daddy! Don't stay outside!

And he bent so that his head was between his legs and waited for the world to disappear in a big wind, like his father said, as he hid among the body bags, the gas masks, the dehydrated and canned food, the evacuation procedures, afraid and small in the dark. An hour passed, maybe three or four. No flash. No wind. Maybe it was a silent bomb, and he'd have to check outside to see if it had landed or maybe destroyed another town down the road. And then he heard footsteps, knocking, and his father stood in the breach and took Harry and hugged him tightly in the ointment of sunlight through the trapdoor.

Harry eased off on the gas pedal as he smelled the aftershave, felt the bristles of his father's beard against his cheeks, heard his father tell him for the hundredth time: The bomb will make everything you ever knew go away—your friends—nothing left at all.

And young Harry Dietz wanted to know what losing everything might feel like but got a headache from trying.

Someone flashed their headlights right at his bumper and he pulled off the highway, narrowly missing an eighteen-wheeler as the driver jammed his brakes. The long sound of a blasting horn and the smell of burning rubber. No wonder those people had been so frantic earlier on the highway, putting on makeup and reading the newspaper while they were driving. They had to keep moving, keep up to date.

There, a phone in that station. The 800 number: he remembered it.

Yes, folks, and now we have a Mr. Dietz calling from a payphone in the Chicago area.

Yes, this is Mr. Dietz.

Go ahead, sir. Your question.

Where did you say these Russians were?

The other man said, I said they're in Montana, secret training camps, funded by the United Nations.

Harry breathed into the handset as he tried to understand the magnitude of the situation.

Caller, do you have another question?

I can't see any Russians. I've been driving for most of the day and I didn't see one of them.

You're making fun of our guest, Mr. Dietz—

—and what are they wearing? I want to be able to see them coming. I don't want to be caught off guard.

Caller—

Have they landed in the past few hours? How come I heard nothing about this, and how come nobody's doing anything about it? I don't want to be captured.

You won't be laughing soon, Mr. Dietz.

The host's words swung in the handset as Dietz ran to his car. The highway brought him to the Chicago skyline, and he followed the traffic until the road split around elevated train tracks. He drew to a stop on a well-lit street near the river and walked along the pavement, his bathrobe blowing in a stiff breeze. He'd sleep in the car tonight, get a job tomorrow, and try to stay ahead of the Russians.

A doorman stared from the entrance to a carpeted lobby as Harry approached. An arm with a red band on the sleeve blocked him. You can't come in here.

I just want to get warm.

No. A second arm.

What's the world coming to when I can't get warm?

When the doorman threatened to call the police, Harry went back to his car and stretched out on the front seat, tired from the driving. He wondered what time it was. Perhaps he had already been sleeping in the car. And then a good mood charged at him in a moment of glory: weeks now since he'd been fired, but worth it just to have seen that mean bastard Beodeker's face turn pale on the day he got fired when he, Harry Dietz, leaned into Beodeker's office and screamed at him that just because he was the damn boss it didn't give him the right to steal another man's girl all those years ago, and that just because Mary Norman was now his wife still hadn't given her the right to sneak around and steal a dead man's smell. Harry lay on the seat and remembered the silence in the store, the way the cops came and escorted him out, the sick way everyone stared as Beodeker walked behind him saying, Fired, you're fired.

Harry shivered. It was cold here. He watched the evening crowds slide by his windshield, heard snatches of conversation, laughter, music blaring as pub doors opened. He felt the carton of milk: it reassured him, and then he thought of Fred.

When he woke it was still dark. He gasped and sat up. The car was parked under a sidewalk tree, and birds coiled themselves around the branches in bursts. Harry held his breath, waiting for familiar things to reveal themselves. He groped his way out of the car and walked the pavement, holding his robe tightly against the wind.

Harry Dietz strained back to look up at the city lights reflecting off the skyscraper windows, each one telling him a different story. One told him he was cold, another said he was hungry, another said he was a boy, another said it didn't recognize him at all. Then they all got together and said nothing at all. He strained to listen for the sound of the 78s—Caruso, the big bands—and for the smell of cigarette smoke, and for his dad to appear out of one of those windows, waving at him.

The bright windows of the shops. He paused at an electronics store window and checked the display. The glass flashed blues and whites. He watched the shapes emerge from the lights, and he shoved both hands deep into his gown pockets. Shapes coming out of the lights. Russians. The radio man was right, and now it was too late.

He said, Okay, you've got me.

One of the shapes said, The doorman called us.

Your English is very good for a couple of Russians, Harry said.

The other shape took his left arm. Let's get you to the station, friend.

The desk sergeant glanced at the officers, then at Harry, and pointed with her pen to a chair. After a few minutes, one of the officers sat beside him.

We made some calls, Mr. Dietz. We traced your plates. You're from Charleston. We're waiting for a call from the police there. They'll see if anyone can pick you up.

Fine.

The officer left and the desk sergeant's pen scratched the silence from the air. Harry pointed to the wide shelf on the wall behind her.

A Zenith.

The desk sergeant said without looking up, Very good. My dad gave it to me.

That's a 1967 Zenith, seven tubes, model N731, I think.

She turned to the radio. You know, I think that's right. You can see that from there?

I used to work with radios. It's got an aerial built-in for both AM and FM, so you'll get a good sound, even in here.

I used to get the local stations when it wasn't busy. But it stopped working. Haven't listened to it in a while.

Your father bought a good model. He knew his radios.

She left her pen on the table. Yes, he did. Then she smiled at the man in the gown and the moccasins. Would you like some coffee?

Do you have milk?

Officer Kearns poured Mr. Dietz a hot mug in the staff canteen. Another cop dropped his hat on the table and sat down, pulled out a notebook from his breast pocket.

I need to be at home. Got this cold coming on.

Don't we all, she said.

She wondered why he still worked as a cop. Every evening, same line. I should really be at home. *Go home then.*

Jane, the guy in the gown.

That's Mr. Dietz. He's lost, I think. From Charleston. We're getting hold of his neighbors.

Well he was tinkering with that old radio of yours. Said something about a loose tube.

She backed into the swinging door.

Mr. D   ? Did you fix my radio?

He was not where she had left him. Officer Kearns stood in the waiting room and heard The Drifters.

Mr. Dietz?

She looked at the shelf on which her father's Zenith was playing for the first time in eighteen years, since he switched it on in the evenings in the seventies after he came home and tapped her head with his newspaper, saying, How's my sweetie?

But she'd been gone barely long enough to boil the water.

Sitting in the back row of the movies on a Saturday night with you.

Mr. Dietz?

The radio sounded like new, tinny but warm. The dials looked big and confident, and the dust that found the tiny crevices in the grille mattered now—she took a tissue from her pocket and spat on it, wiped the film off. And when the warm brown wood shone back at her, she stood again in her living room, with her dad relaxing after work, fiddling with the radio. She heard her friends singing on the bus home, felt the hot pavement underneath her feet on Saturday mornings. She tasted the orange ice pop on her tongue when she slid the taste along it, cold and sweet on those hot days. She heard the silence when he left without notice, drove a car away to work, and work became five o'clock, and work became seven o'clock, and the calls, and the police, and the silence of the line when she lifted the phone to see if her dad would answer. Months later, her mother's finger twirling the phone line as if coaxing it into ringing. Her hand on the hairbrush that caught a few strands in the corner of the bathroom mirror. Opening the cabinet. Pills on her palm, on her tongue, in her saliva, in her throat, in her eyes.

She learned that some people want to disappear, and there's no finding them after that. The world is full of the missing. She saw her mother from then on only in bits and pieces, in mirrors, in the car, closing the door to her bedroom. And her father? A face in Vancouver, a credit card handed to a supermarket clerk in Portland, an envelope with ten-dollar bills now and then.

And the radio? The sound died and the dust arrived with tiny suitcases. The silent Zenith turned into a large apartment block of wires settled by dust, decorated by dust, silenced by dust. A whole country of radio dust with elected officials, a dust government, a parliament of dust, the dust halls of power, the congress of dust calling dust to order.

Harry was careful as he walked the streets. The black was on him once more. He dug his hands into the robe pockets and kept it from blowing about as he rounded the corner and blended in with the crowd. A child pointed, Look at that man in the red gown.

He slouched along on the pavement, shoulders hunched to hide his face. Behind him a loudspeaker corded the sky. Clear the way! Move your vehicle! He held his dressing gown up a couple of inches and looked behind him at the sirens. Ahead of him, a woman carried a child down a hole.

His breath ran frosted ahead of him and he couldn't catch up with it until he came to the hole and stopped. More people going into it, some running, some apparently not that concerned, but all down the stairs to the bomb shelter: he followed them, not daring to look behind as the steps darkened and his hand on the railings became his eyes. At the bottom a tunnel appeared ahead. Everyone walked at a steady pace, and Harry admired their composure: these people had been well trained by their parents. He too walked without hurry. Some read a newspaper as they walked, doubtless, Harry thought, so that they could hide their faces as they approached safety. He held up his right hand and studied it, where he used to write the answers to the questions. This provided an ounce of privacy. Got to blend in with the crowd. He followed until the people around him were silhouettes in the growing light ahead. Then everyone bunched up. Harry held his breath: he did not like people pressing him like this. He watched people place something into the slot and move through a revolving gate, down some short stairs. He felt around in his pocket and pulled out a couple of dollars, then joined the line for a window where a man who never looked up took the money and pushed a coin back. Harry placed the money down, said nothing like everyone else and took his coin.

He stood at the gate and dropped the cc   he slot.
Just then a gush of cool air bathed his face and   heard the
whine of metal hitting metal. He tried to mo   backward
but the revolving bars wouldn't go backwards, and the man
behind him who carried a small black suitcase in his left
hand shouted, Come on!

Harry saw the crush ahead, saw some people emerging
from the interior, trying to get out through the bars, and they
stood in front of him. He was caught between both sides. If
they were trying to get out, that meant it was dangerous in
there. He turned to the man behind him.

I'm going back. Please, tell the man in the window to
make this go backwards.

Someone shouted, Tell that guy to move.

Hey, you in the gown, we got a life to get to.

The man with the small black suitcase said, You can't
go back.

What?

You can't go back. The suitcase was up. Clear the way.

Harry put the coin in and went with the crowd: they
came to a moving stairs going farther underground. A very
extensive shelter, this. Question was, how long would he
have to wait for the all-clear? He moved to the edge of the
platform and looked down the tracks.

Very tired. Would like to go to bed now. His heart
moved in his chest like a lizard he'd once caught as a boy
that dug into his palm with little darts of toes before he let
it go. He closed his eyes and thought of Fred. The wind
again, but cool and pleasant. The screech, when it came,
made him shout and he staggered back to the wall and hid
his face. A train slid out of the tunnel, a long, long train.

Harry shuffled through the doors. All the seats were taken, and as the train moved off he held a strap, just as everyone else standing did. Some looked at the ground, some at the pictures on the walls, some at a book, some listened to radios through earphones. The rest found a place with no people to rest their eyes. Harry tapped a young boy on the shoulder. The boy took the earphones off.

What?

Harry leaned close, What's the situation?

What?

How long will we be here, do you think?

The boy put the earphones back on. Harry nodded.

Don't worry. It's been this way for years. I did this as a child.

A woman got up and Harry took her place because he was tired. When she left, Harry took her copy of the *Chicago Tribune* and read the headline:

Terrorist Threat: City in Fear.

Harry scanned what he could of the smaller headlines underneath: Vice-President says the threat is real, terrorists with nuclear weapons. Harry saw the flash of the bomb and felt the match flaring up and felt the pain again. It searched his body with wiry fingers and pressed on his arms and then dug its nails all in one place.

More people rose for the following stop. Then there was just Harry and a girl sitting at the other end of the car. When the girl left her seat, Harry got off too. The girl's footsteps clicking on the tiles ahead. She turned out of sight. Harry followed her through long halls and up a long moving set of steps, felt cooler air on his skin, saw the tops of buildings. He was back on the street and it was still night. He gripped his gown and walked past the girl who stopped and watched him go by. It was a pity that people couldn't talk freely. But anyone could be a Russian.

He passed dark alleyways in which fires burned out of barrels that men stood around, drinking. Buildings with parts of walls missing and cracked windows. It was obvious that a bomb must have landed on them. Harry heard a sharp report and ducked, felt a mixture of excitement and fear. Some people were still fighting. Real heroes, people holding out in the dark. A siren moved across the night.

His right ankle grew hot. Harry took his eyes from the sky and forgot why he had been searching it for so long.

Well look at you. He leaned down and petted the cat as it twined around his ankle and he felt the heat on the other leg.

Want to come home with me? He picked it up. It leaned into his chest and he stroked its head. I have some milk for you, little kitty. Well, not here, but later, when I get home.

You're lucky she didn't scratch your eyes right out of your head.

Harry turned to a child holding a doll. She pointed to the cat.

That's Moses. She's a street cat. She fights lots of cats all the time. Even dogs.

Hello Moses, Harry said. Strange name for a girl cat.

The girl said, Moses doesn't care. And I've never seen Moses in anyone's arms before. Not even once. You must be a cat-man or something. A man once kicked Moses, and my daddy and another man had to get her off his face because she jumped up and hung onto his face off her nails, like this. The girl put her hands into claws and brought them together in a vice grips. It took a while and the man cried.

Harry let the cat down.

Dietz is the name. He held out his hand but she stepped back. Harry Dietz. And who might you be, young lady?

Mildred.

Well, Mildred, I'm hungry and I am going back to my apartment. And by the way, what are you doing out on a night like this with all this fighting going on?

My apartment is too small, and anyway, my mom and dad have been fighting since I can remember.

My god. What age are you now?

Ten years and four months.

So it's been that long, Harry thought. One parent against another. Probably a language problem. One parent can't understand a word the other says.

Mildred, he said, I wouldn't worry too much if I were you. And not a child like you, as pretty as you.

Easy for you to say, Mildred said.

Why is that?

You're lost, aren't you?

A little bit, Harry said.

Mildred looked around her and widened her eyes.

More than a little bit, Harry. You are lost a big bit. You are a whole lot of lost.

I'm a stick, not a boomerang, Harry said.

What? Mildred brought the doll close to her ear. She listened, head cocked, took a deep breath, and said, Harry, she says you better get out of here fast.

Why is that?

Mildred turned and pointed.

A large man walked up to them. He wore glasses and a cardigan. Mildred, there you are. Where have you been? Hey, who are you? What you doing with my Mildred?

He's okay, Dad. He's lost, that's all.

Is that what the man said to you, Mildred?

No.

What then?

He picked up Moses and nothing happened.

The man walked up to Harry and pointed his finger across the city.

Get lost back to where you came from, old man. Be lost in your own place. You can't get lost here.

Harry said, Did something explode around here?

Okay, we got ourselves a mouth. The man shoved Harry against a post, bunched Harry's collar in his fist. Talking with my daughter.

Dad, Mildred said.

Be quiet! Where are you now, old man? Are you in your own place now?

No, Harry said.

Dad, he's lost. Moses likes him.

Harry felt the grip loosen. Moses? the man said.

Harry picked up Moses.

The man looked sideways at Harry Dietz, then at Moses. I'm guessing you're the luckiest man this side of the city.

I'm just lost.

Here's what we're going to do, lost man. He lifted his thumb. Mildred, you get back inside, and I mean now. And you, I'm going to bring you out of here.

Five minutes later a beige Lincoln Continental drove up. The man motioned Harry in. The door wouldn't close right for Harry, and the man ended up getting out again, kicking it hard and shouting at the same time.

He got in and they pulled away. This is a huge car, Harry said.

The way it was in 1979. So tell me about Moses. How come she didn't cut you up? I can't touch that cat and she lives in my house.

I picked her up.

Just like that? That cat will not let me come close, even when I'm putting the food in her bowl.

I hear she's got a temperament.

Did Mildred use that word?

No, she said about fighting.

Did she now?

They drove through another three traffic lights in silence until Harry finally couldn't take it any longer and said, Do you do a lot of fighting? Is that something you can talk about?

The man looked at Harry and swung the car over to the side of the road.

I don't know what Mildred's been saying to you, but there's no fighting in my house.

Then Mildred must be very proud of you and your wife if you've been fighting for most of her life. She must be very proud of you both indeed.

The man looked away and laughed. Look, Mildred imagines a lot of things. He took a drag of his cigarette and blew smoke against where he pointed. See that tower a few blocks that way? We're at the edge of the neighborhood here. Just keep walking that way and don't look back.

Harry followed the man's finger.

Just keep that tower dead ahead of you and you'll be back in your own place soon enough. You got that, old man?

Harry got out and slammed the door. It swung open as the car squealed into a circle.

He followed the lights that lit the sky above where the man had pointed. More lights in that part of the city. He kept the tower in sight and walked close to the walls, in case any fighting erupted around him. The breeze lifted his gown as he passed a bright window on the edge of a busy street. The flashing sign said DINER. He was under the tower. Inside the diner, a thin woman sat by the window writing on a notepad with one hand while scanning the street with binoculars.

Just the person he needed. She might know some things. Looked about eighty. Could help him get back to his apartment and get the television working.

He waved back at the dark part of the city in case the man was watching. Thank you.

He walked inside to conversations, Sinatra on the loudspeakers, heat on the swish of his legs inside the gown, and approached his reflection in the window behind her table with a question: Are you from around here?

We're all from around here, she said.

I'm Harry Dietz, I'm from Ireland.

Good for you, she said under the binoculars.

Harry felt sorry for her, another woman trying to survive. He went to the counter and raised his hand until the young waitress saw him. I'd like a coffee.

What kind of coffee?

A mug.

She rolled her eyes up and blew hair off her forehead.

Would you like regular or decaf is what I mean.

He pointed to the woman's table, Just black. I'm over there.

She rolled her eyeballs again. Maybe she had a disease, had to go around rolling her eyeballs every minute.

I wouldn't worry about that eye problem. It will pass.

She stared at him, called back to the counter, Two coffees!

I only want one, Harry said.

She always gets a second, the waitress said.

Harry returned to the table and sat down. I took a wrong turn, and I'm finding my way back.

Aren't we all, the woman said.

He drank his coffee and looked out the window. The diner light flashed. He thought about Mildred and Moses. It was a good thing for him that Moses liked him. Harry felt his face and imagined Moses' claws in his eyeballs and then, in the middle of all that pain, trying to pull the cat off his face, then not being able to get the cat off and asking for help from passersby with the cat on his face. The woman sipped from her coffee and trained the binoculars on a building across the street. Then she wrote on her pad. She noticed Harry watching her.

I'm minding my own business, she said. Do you mind?

I understand. Then he whispered, You've got to keep ahead of them. I was sent here by a man.

The woman's face brightened. A man sent you here?

He said I should come to the tower.

She clapped her hands. I didn't think he was interested,

thought I was a pest making all those complaints. You never know with the police.

Harry said yes because he wanted to be polite and keep the woman happy. If she were happy, she might make him happy.

I've got something for you, she said and moved beside him. Harry lifted the mug to his lips. This was good coffee. But no pills.

The woman shoved page three of the *Chicago Tribune* under Harry's face. In case you don't already know, my name is Phyllis.

Hello, Phyllis. Harry Dietz.

Harry, listen to this. Phyllis put her finger on the page and read from it:

And in the park, a fourth woman assaulted in four weeks. The victim described the man to police as about sixty years old and tall, who asked her the time as she walked on the park's main trail. She said that he spoke in a gentlemanly fashion before jumping on her. He wore a loose white shirt and green trousers, with a sweater draped around his hips.

Phyllis said, What I'm saying is, I called the police because I think I know who's doing this.

Harry lifted the mug again. His coffee was a little cool and he wanted more. He looked at the waitress leaning over the counter reading a pink magazine.

Phyllis said, Mr. Hugh Greene, late of the state of California, who appeared in my apartment block four months ago with barely half a van of furniture and belongings. In fact, one armchair was all the furniture Mr. Greene brought with him.

One armchair, Harry said.

What kind of man brings one armchair to Chicago? she said.

That's a bit strange.

The rest of what Mr. Greene brought was clothes, a set of golf clubs, three large bags, and fifteen large boxes. I heard from the van driver that the boxes contained mostly books, though there were also many photographs of Greene's family—a woman and children and what may have been grandchildren.

Grandchildren, Harry said.

Now the van driver told me what Mr. Greene told *him* on the trip to Chicago, because Mr. Greene drove with him in the van and talked about his family.

Mr. Greene talked about his family, Harry said.

Evidently Greene met his wife in England when he was training for the invasion of Normandy. Which would make Greene eighty years old.

That's interesting, Harry said.

He went to Harvard after the war. Became a lawyer, made a fortune.

Harry kept his eyes open because he wanted to find the right moment to ask the woman where they were now in relation to his apartment above the Shaws. He should listen to her story first, it was polite to do that. He often listened to people at work.

She said, Then I find out that Greene's wife is dead, and his children live overseas. So this man, she said, this rich man comes from California to our apartment block.

Seems that way, Harry said. He watched the waitress wet her fingertip and flip a page.

Phyllis leaned over and spoke in a pointed whisper. But this isn't a place where rich people go, she said. And anyway, after a wife dies—she leaned low and whispered with her hand cupped around her mouth—what kind of man brings one armchair to Chicago?

Though tired now, Harry closed his eyes as if listening, a trick he learned at Beodeker's.

So I decided to observe Mr. Greene; his apartment is opposite mine, so I leave the door open a chink. He never suspects a thing. Always greets me in the hallway, asks me about my family, always questions.

He likes to talk, Harry said.

Phyllis opened a notebook where she had written, she said, some very precise observations:

He leaves every morning between 8:00 and 8:45 for this coffee shop, stays here, reads the morning paper until about eleven. He sits near the counter and talks with the staff. Seems popular. I ask my friends at the weekly card game to help with surveillance. I outline my suspicions. I don't feel comfortable with a new man on the floor. These days, I tell them, you never know. In fact, the first assault happened in the park six weeks after Mr. Greene's delivery van pulled up outside the apartments. He was out of his apartment at the time. I tell them I spoke with a Detective Murray, who advised me to lock my door. Greene is a suspect, my friends agree, based on his strange behavior: his offers to carry their groceries, his sudden presence when they can't find their keys, wanting to help, his requests to play gin rummy on Friday nights, his white hair, his watery eyes, his general lack of family. How he paces at night.

The woman drank from her cup and said, Well, what do you think?

Harry said, He's your man.

Imagine, a man in his eighties that driven.

Harry searched for his pills in his gown pocket. Maybe they were in his jacket— he could drive back to the diner in case that young boy John felt guilty enough to bring it back.

Phyllis got up. I have to leave. Mr. Greene may be watching.

As Phyllis left, the waitress glanced up. Harry caught her eye and lifted his mug.

She waved the bill: You'll be paying for the coffees?

No, I don't think so. Don't have any money, not with me, anyway.

Harry noticed that this time the young woman's eyes did not roll up but stayed on him.

Eric, she said.

A man came out of the kitchen with a towel draped across his left shoulder.

Says he doesn't have any money. Four coffees.

I only had one, Harry said.

The waitress said, Your lady friend had three. You wait here.

She and Eric bent to the cash register. Harry stood and left, heard Eric shout. Outside Harry looked up along the high pavement of windows, the walls of skyscrapers, where every dark frame was a story missing. The city was getting lost. I'm waiting, come find me, Dad, come get me before you cannot find me in the dark. I cannot help you then.

VISIT

THE FIRST WEEKEND IN APRIL began cloudy but broke into splinters of sunlight and gusts by afternoon on the Friday. I had driven the hundred or so miles from Galway to the nursing home that housed almost thirty residents, a recently-built long T-shaped bungalow on the outskirts of Mullingar, and walked the long hall and read the book of familiar pages through open doors: the eyes that looked for someone familiar, and failing that, for a conversation. Those eyes held voices and followed you until you passed and sometimes called after you. I could not breathe my way along that hall. When I came to her door it was open as always, but slightly, and her face filled the narrow space; she was asleep, but lightly, and when I opened it wider, an expression I knew filled in the dormant spaces of that face with the person I knew. Left to their own devices, a few months alone can drain people of themselves, but here she was, and still herself. I bent to kiss her forehead.

A nurse looked into the room, smiled at me and closed the door. My mother turned her head on the pillow to the box of Cadbury's chocolates by the television.

Take one, Luke, there's plenty of them.

I adjusted the pillow at her neck. She lived in the armchair now because she was afraid of lying on her back, what would happen, how she might suffocate, never rise again. At a certain stage illness must take a shape and a name and move into the room with the sick, preferring a particular corner, and utterly silent, wait with an equal malaise. So she watched too and slept in the armchair, ate in it, and the pillow gave her little comfort, but she was lost without something to put behind her. At night the nurses piled a couple more on a footstool to elevate her legs. That was the routine. I wondered what thoughts occupy a body for months in an armchair when there's nothing to fan them away, no distraction, no business elsewhere. They must crowd close.

She asked me to open a window and we watched a show on the television before both falling asleep in the sharp light. I still hadn't recovered from the jet lag and woke after her, an hour or so later. She saw me move and laughed.

Looks like we were both out for the count.

I was out alright. I noticed that the sun had crept to the top corner of the window.

She turned, It's a lovely day.

A little over a long time had quickened to a lot over a short time. A few of our neighbors, the ones who made the trip from Galway to visit her, sometimes met in the hall, and I once heard them whisper how she looked so different recently. I wondered why people whispered when they wanted to keep things secret since whispers draw far more attention than ordinary speech. Who wants to listen to people talk? But whispers, now that must be important. I played my own part in the passage: I checked on her health with the nurses on the way out each time, and they answered, sometimes without looking up: She's fine and comfortable, which is what they said about every resident in the home. These are the best answers to the questions people ask to make themselves feel comfortable before they open the doors back to the sunlight and the fresh air of their own lives, the town they live in that is far away from there. A nursing home is after all a business: if you run one you want people sending their own parents there in time. You want people to leave feeling that they have done all they can, because it is all a question of time.

I said to her, Do you want to go out?

She laughed. I haven't been out in ages. Months.

I opened the window and checked for clouds. Well it's fine out, I said.

Okay then, she said.

I went down the hall and told the nurse on duty that I wanted to take my mother for a walk. I could see the nurse taking it in. She asked questions and answered them herself.

A walk? You mean outside to the lawn? Under the tree? Yes, we'll be right there.

Escape is also a matter of time. At a certain age and when the cities of the body no longer accept emissaries and require advance notice for anything, movement becomes a ritual like a king's procession, it builds into ceremonies of delay, whether to the bathroom or to the window, both of which are thousands of miles away. I waited in the lounge in front of the loud television while two nurses removed her from the armchair, dressed her, placed her in a wheelchair, and handed her the small plastic purse without which she would not leave. Twenty minutes later they brought her in a cardigan to the door of the waiting room. A blanket covered her legs, the smile had always been there.

Now there, she's ready, one of them said. Enjoy your walk, Mary.

I stood behind and wheeled her outside the building as we moved from shade to the bright late afternoon.

Where do you want to go? I said. Over there, by the tree?

Let's go out the gate, she said.

Out the gate—you mean out onto the road? I said.

Why not.

A car tore by. It was the busy route from the west into Mullingar.

Right or left?

Right, towards town.

The town center was a mile along the freshly tarred road, and there was no pavement to it yet but flattened piles of stones from the construction, probably because no one was expected to be walking along it. I wheeled her beyond the white wall and immediately the wheelchair sank an inch into gravel that lined the edge for about a hundred yards. Up ahead a hard shoulder waited, but not here, and to the side of the gravel the high, untended grass pocked the dirt mounds. Back in the fields lay the undiscovered foundations of many houses to come, the rough magic of building sites, the cold cauldron of pools and cement.

I think the tires are a bit light on air, I said, and dug my legs in for purchase and a sustained push to get the wheelchair moving; by coming at it from either side and shoving hard onto the handles or lifting them, I was able to shift it onto the harder mix of dry clay and stones. I felt the sun and sweat on my neck, remembered when I worked in gardens, and wondered why I hadn't done that in so long, the smell of a lifted shovel and clay, the promise of flowers, what you bury that soon waves effortlessly in the wind. We were moving now. Three cars sped by us in a group, and the breeze lifted the blanket off her legs.

I saw her nightdress under the cardigan. Are you cold?

Not at all, I'm fine. Let's keep going.

I leaned down and pushed in the right place. A little rocking along the uneven surface and jammed rocks held us back, but after five minutes—about a hundred yards—we reached the hard-shoulder section and moved easier until we passed where the river came close to the road. The water creased into a fan and we watched the white of a swan filter through the reeds. It did not weigh anything. A red wildflower leaned out of the grass on a stem that held it above the weeds. A bird sang from nearby, close enough to be invisible, and I didn't recognize the type of song. Perhaps for once the flower was singing and the bird was a blade of grass.

So keep going? I said.

Yes.

Another few hundred yards and the traffic thickened, people glancing out of their cars at this man pushing a woman along a road in a wheelchair, nothing but blank faces in glass fleeting by with glances that could be read in that instant, what this must be, what is happening, why is that woman on the road and who is that man and where could they be going; but they drove steadily on under the shifting cloud of the late afternoon sky, probably because others were following right behind. Rolling easily on the smooth surface and picking up to walking speed I felt her weight in my hands, yet my hands held no weight. We were two parts of an enterprise only a half mile from town, and the going was good from there until we reached the first path and soon after that came to a petrol station, the briquettes stacked, the gas containers chained, the sign for prices, the first locals buying milk and bread.

I slowed. I'm going to put some air in the tires. Is that okay?

That's fine.

I wheeled her into the station past the petrol pumps, past the shop and across to the machine off at the side where you put in your coin; a car stopped to let us pass—I waved thanks and lined the wheelchair up and waited as my mother found a coin in her purse, then fitted the hose to the valve of the right wheel, ratcheting until I heard the air sizzle like a morning fry. A man filling his tank gave us a second, a third turn of the head. Another car slowed as it pulled out, two faces stuck like old questions to the right rear window. When the first wheel felt firm, I filled the other. She looked ahead.

That's better, I said.

Meanwhile the entire station became one face that watched a woman in a wheelchair getting some air. It was possible that they did not see me as I was bent down to the wheel. Yes, a lady of some years had apparently stopped for air. As we rolled out of the station, wheels hard and ready for town, the attendant signaled out at us from the line of customers, his face connecting a laugh and a question in the recognition or hope that shows itself whenever something different comes your way and releases the handle of the ordinary. It was the closest anyone came to a word.

I was glad to be moving again. Even April can be chilly.

Visit

I said, Are we still going into town?

I think so. Feels much better, she said.

We made a left and reached a row of houses, and half an hour after we left the gate of the nursing home we passed a sweet shop on the other side of the main street in Mullingar. I pulled the wheelchair to the side to give my arms a rest. We were in the countryside of the town now, and people walked with shopping bags, stood aside and said, Good Day.

I said, Would you like something?

She pulled the purse from under her blanket again. Not really, but you get something for yourself.

No, I've got enough.

She held out a wad of notes. Here, Luke. And get me some jelly babies.

She said she would be okay, and the chair was parallel to the road and not on any kind of slope. I folded the money and locked the wheels, crossed the road and walked into dark aisles of a small shop looking for jelly babies, stepping carefully and palming the packets for detail in the dark, like a cinema. The bags and wrappers rustled under my fingers, the same food that had passed a hundred playtimes and to which a hundred times we bent in rows of desks at school, slipping in a sweet under a teacher's gaze with a flick of the finger, then back up with the head to myths or triangles, whatever it was. The dim containers woke as my eyes got used to the light and recited their names: wine gums, jelly babies, fruit pastilles. I held a bag up to smell it.

Is that everything?

I looked behind me to the boy with the question who lingered at the cash register looking down the aisle at me. He had asked well, the right mix of suspicion and help. I waited at the counter as he rang me up and slid the coins out, placing them before me in a small stack. Outside I saw her sitting in the wheelchair, hands folded on her lap, and knew I was living the moment that says nothing, that will allow nothing said of consequence. I walked out of the shop and to the edge of the road, waited for the traffic to pass, holding the change she would insist I keep.

The cars kept coming. It was getting on in the day and after work. Dinners were ready, lights flooding rooms. The afternoon dramas like *Emmerdale Farm* were at an end, and soon it would be time for the news.

I looked again and put a foot out to cross but stepped back as more cars like black and red drops rose out of the nowhere at one end of the street and slid to the nowhere at the other end, each hiding her a second so that she disappeared and appeared like a film on reel. Then the string of traffic passed and the way was clear, and though it was time, I held the sweets and the change and still waited to cross.

My mother faced west where the sky breached the uneven rooftops and the early evening light pressed the orange doors of the houses. She was smiling. Her eyes were closed and her face was calm, turned to the sun.

THE END

ACKNOWLEDGMENTS

T HIS COLLECTION TOOK fifteen years to write. Some of the stories date from the early nineties, some transformed themselves in time, and a couple are new. And as with any writing-in-progress, the shape and purpose changed. Along the way I was fortunate to receive advice from the following: Stephen Dixon, John Yount, Colum McCann, Jay Prefontaine, Graham Lewis, and Christina Nalty. I thank my agent, Jin Auh, and my editor, David Shoemaker. I want to pay my respects also to two people whose support and words of encouragement came at vital times: The generous voice that charged Larry Brown's own fiction was no invention—he was that voice—and David Marcus, whose love and support for the Irish short story afforded a platform for my writing.

"Morning Swimmers" and "How Long Until" appeared in *Granta*; "Glass" in *Phoenix Irish Short Stories 2003* and *The Recorder*; "Harry Dietz" in *The Faber Book of Best New Irish Short Stories 2004-2005*; and "The Visit" in *Vrij Nederland* and *The Recorder*.